W9-BWS-153

The Papercutter

Book 1 of The Split Trilogy

Copyright © 2021 by Cindy Rizzo

Bella Books, Inc.
P.O. Box 10543
Tallahassee, FL 32302

All rights reserved. No part of this book may be reproduced or transmitted in any form or by any means, electronic or mechanical, including photocopying, without permission in writing from the publisher.

This is a work of fiction. Names, characters, businesses, places, events and incidents are either the products of the author's imagination or used in a fictitious manner. Any resemblance to actual persons, living or dead, or actual events is purely coincidental. The publisher does not have any control over and does not assume any responsibility for author or third-party websites or their content.

Printed in the United States of America on acid-free paper.

First Bella Books Edition 2021

Editor: Katherine V. Forrest
Cover Designer: Kayla Mancuso

ISBN: 978-1-64247-247-9

PUBLISHER'S NOTE

The scanning, uploading, and distribution of this book via the Internet or via any other means without the permission of the publisher is illegal and punishable by law. Please purchase only authorized electronic editions, and do not participate in or encourage electronic piracy of copyrighted materials. Your support of the author's rights is appreciated.

The Papercutter

Book 1 of The Split Trilogy

Cindy Rizzo

Fountaindale Public Library District
300 W. Briarcliff Rd.
Bolingbrook, IL 60440

BELLA
BOOKS

2021

For Naomi, Natalie & Nina Weinberg

Who deserve to live in a country that is worthy of them.

"Some stories are true that never happened."

-Elie Wiesel

THE SPLIT

After decades of increasing polarization, the United States of America became ungovernable and split itself into two nations. Each state joined one of the new countries—the God Fearing States of America (GFS), a majority white Christian conservative nation; and the United Progressive Regions of America (UPR), a majority nonwhite, liberal nation.

Except Ohio, which was divided in two.

CHAPTER ONE

Judith

Cincinnati, South Ohio, God Fearing States

We don't see them until we turn the corner and then it's too late. Hannah grabs my hand and pulls me into a run. I turn my head and see three red hats emblazoned with GFB gaining on us.

We crouch down behind the hedges at the back of our school. The sound of heavy footfalls in pursuit suddenly stops and we know they are nearby looking for us.

"Little Jew girls," one of them calls out in a singsong voice. "Come out so you can see our new decoration on the wall of your Jew school."

There's laughter and then a second voice calls out, "C'mon, they're not worth us getting caught. Probably smell bad anyway."

"Who's gonna catch us? The cops hate them as much as we do."

Now their laughter sounds farther away, which means they might be leaving. Hannah slowly stands to peer over the hedge and I tug her down, afraid they'll turn and discover us.

"They're going," she whispers in my ear. We wait a little longer and then walk slowly in the opposite direction, back toward the side entrance of our school where we'd first seen them.

"Look, there!" I exclaim, pointing to the white brick wall of our school's side entrance. The graffiti is scrawled in black paint, the letters dripping in a way that makes me think of ads I've seen for horror movies. *Jew Scum Out of GFS!* I clutch the sleeve of Hannah's blouse.

"It'll be gone by lunchtime," she says, annoyance clear in her voice. "I'm surprised they aren't out here already with their magic paint remover pretending this never happened."

This is the third one we've seen in the last week, though it's the first time we actually caught the GFB, the so-called God Fearing Boys, in the act. Not that we actually caught them since we were the ones running for our lives.

And while I hate everything they stand for, they're right about one thing. The police likely know who they are but will not do anything to stop them.

There seems to be more graffiti showing up in our neighborhood as GFS Independence Day approaches. Who knows how much has been cleaned up so fast that we've never gotten to see it?

Hannah snaps a photo with her device. "Well at least now no one can say that this never happened."

She's amassed a collection of hateful graffiti, all of it threatening our community if we don't leave the country. When she showed some of them to her father, he just shrugged. "This is what our people have endured for centuries, and yet we're still here. Don't worry, little Hannahla. Just be good in school and listen to your mother. The best thing you can do to help our people survive is to marry a nice boy and bring many Jewish children into the world."

Despite similar responses from my father, neither Hannah nor I have been able to turn our backs and pretend we haven't seen what we're seeing. The problem is, we have no idea what to do about it. Maybe our fathers are right and there is nothing we can do. After all, we're just two seventeen-year-old girls trying to survive our meaningless time in high school. Still, it feels like it's getting worse and I can't help but worry.

We continue walking toward the side entrance of our school. We know from experience it isn't a good idea to spend too much time looking at the graffiti. A few weeks ago, Manny the janitor caught us and screamed that we had no business being there. Then he marched us into Mrs. Feldman's office. It happened so fast, all we could do was stare at the floor and mumble an apology to the principal who seems to think that looking at the graffiti is more of a crime than actually spraying the stuff on the wall.

I stop when we reach the concrete steps in front of the entrance. "Hannah, do you think it's safe to keep those pictures on your device? It wouldn't be too difficult for somebody to figure out what you're doing."

She steps sideways to get closer to me and speaks softly into my ear. "I've been uploading them to one of those little memory dots and hiding it someplace safe."

I shake my head. "But why save them when nobody thinks they're a big deal?"

I feel her breath on the side of my face as she lets out a sigh. "I don't know, Judith. I guess I need to hold on to something to prove to myself that I'm not going crazy."

* * *

I sit confined in the hardwood classroom desk: an uncomfortable chair attached to a writing surface. Mrs. Kastenbaum is droning on about the history of the God Fearing States. When I stare directly at her, trying to get a fix on her soul, it neither shows up as shimmering with goodness nor hollowed out with malevolence. Unfortunately, not everyone shows their true soul to me. Mine is an imperfect gift from Hashem, the Hebrew word for God we use outside the synagogue. It's a gift that enables me to see the soul, the *neshamah*, of some but not others. Maybe Hashem thinks there's no reason for me to see Mrs. Kastenbaum's soul.

I nudge my notebook to the side and stare at the grain in the wood of my desk. Its horizontal lines vary with each slat of honey-colored wood. I count six along the smooth surface and a seventh at the top with two long indents for pens and pencils. Frustrated by the random nature of the grain, I turn my attention to the design for a papercut I'd started thinking about for the Jewish holiday of Sukkot, our celebration of the annual harvest season. There has to be an image I could use that's more creative than the standard ones of fruits and vegetables or dining in a *sukkah*, the little booths outside where we eat our meals for a week. But what?

"Hannah Goldwyn, the Second Constitutional Convention took place where?" I snap to attention at the mention of my best friend's name.

"Um, Charleston, North Carolina?"

Okay, Hannah is safe.

Eleventh grade marks a decade during which we've had to sit through some form of this lecture. Because tomorrow is GFS Independence Day, all schools—even the religious ones like Kushner Academy for Girls—are required by the government to teach a lesson about the establishment of the country.

When we were younger, they gave us the easy stuff. One year we had to color in the map of the GSF and UPR, red for us and blue for them. I remember thinking I felt bad for the other country because they were separated into two sections. That whole part on the left side, which I later learned is their western region, sits by itself, separated from its blue brothers by a big part of our country. Of course our own state of Alaska is separated, but that is only one state. All the other GFS states form one big red piece from the shore of North Carolina to the border with Mexico, and up to a piece of the border with Canada. Ours is the bigger country.

Mrs. Kastenbaum walks right by my desk, her booming voice shaking me into a state of alert. "And what great doctrine was adopted at the Charleston convention? Yetta?"

Oy, Yetta Freundlich, the insufferable smart aleck who never lets you forget that she knows everything. I'd long ago seen her *neshamah* and since then have kept my distance from that hollowed out soul.

Yetta speaks as if she is the one teaching the class, loud and confident, carefully enunciating each word. "The United States of America adopted the Texas Plan which prohibited the former USA federal government from overturning state laws."

"Correct." Mrs. Kastenbaum pushes out a smile that disappears in a split second. "And what happened in the wake of the assassinations that followed?"

Yetta's hand shoots up, her body straining to catapult out of her seat. I glance over at Hannah who rolls her eyes.

"Oy, okay, Yetta again," says Mrs. Kastenbaum, her voice weary.

"The government canceled the presidential election, and instead the Third Constitutional Convention was held so that the former United States of America could be divided into two new countries." She holds her head erect, looks straight ahead into the distance and continues, her voice even more arrogant than usual. "Our God Fearing States which stand for faith and freedom, and the other one, which stands for atheistic anarchy."

I stop listening and return to planning my papercut, twirling a finger through my dark curly hair. I wonder if I can improve on the design I created last June for Shavuot, the holiday that commemorates when God gave us the Torah. It was the typical image of Moses at the top of Mount Sinai speaking to Hashem. Could a human really stand before God and have an actual conversation? I know it's a death sentence to look Him in the face. But a conversation?

"Judith Braverman, are you with us? Judith!"

Mrs. Kastenbaum's stern voice pulls me off Mount Sinai and back into the classroom. Since I have no idea what I've been asked there is only one thing to do. My body tenses as I take a deep breath.

"Could you please repeat the question?"

Mrs. Kastenbaum sighs, one of those dramatic ones that broadcasts exasperation. "Judith, I won't have inattentiveness in my classroom. Do I make myself clear?"

I nod but am still faced with a steely glare and quickly realize why. I haven't appropriately expressed the right amount of remorse. "Yes, Mrs. Kastenbaum. It won't happen again."

"See that it doesn't or there'll be a demerit and detention."

The glare is gone, replaced by Mrs. Kastenbaum gazing up at the ceiling in thought, her hands behind her back. "Oh yes, now I recall." She looks at me, not quite so steely this time. "What was the Great Migration?"

I exhale with relief because I know the acceptable answer. But I also know about the book that Hannah found hidden in the public library when she was trying to find information for a paper on Jewish immigration to the USA during the early part of the last century. She told me the book she found was wedged against the back of the bookcase, its binding facing the wall. She saw it when she'd pulled out a few books she thought she'd need for her paper and tugged on it until it was free of the bookcase. When she saw that the title mentioned The Great Migration, she thought it had been shelved incorrectly until she took a closer look.

It turned out the book wasn't at all about the two years after The Split when people resettled into the GFS and UPR. It was a book about the migration of Black people from the southern part of the USA to the north during the nineteen hundreds. There was no bar code or sticker from the library on the spine so Hannah wouldn't be able to check it out. It made us wonder if someone had left it there hidden away.

When Hannah snuck the book out of the library and showed it to me later, I first marveled at the beauty of the title, *The Warmth of Other Suns*. But then I suddenly understood the real message of the book.

"So there was another Great Migration before the one after The Split?" I asked.

"Seems so, and it's not too hard to figure out why they never told us about that one."

I nodded, struck by the realization of how little we knew about the people who'd lived in the USA and who had left their homes a second time for the warmth of other suns.

"I've never met anyone Black," I said to Hannah, "have you?"

She shook her head, her long wavy brown hair shifting from left to right and back again. "And we've been told nothing about them or their history."

I fanned the pages of the book listening to the tick-tick-tick of the sounds they made. "I guess we should read this then, right?"

Hannah breathed out her response, "Yeah." She reached over and gently took the book from me. "Makes you wonder what else they're not telling us."

None of what I now know about the original Great Migration can be repeated to Mrs. Kastenbaum if I want to pass her class. Instead, I need to tell her exactly what she wants to hear.

"The Great Migration took place after The Split when people made the decision to settle in either the God Fearing States or the United Progressive Regions."

"And which populations moved where?" she snaps back at me.

"Uh..." I think for a few seconds, deciding it might be best to say something that would get me back into her good graces. "After our country's military put an end to riots and uprisings, they were able to oversee the orderly resettlement of the two new countries. Once it was safe, Orthodox and Hasidic Jews living in parts of the UPR moved to the GFS for religious liberty, as did Evangelical Christians. Then Blacks, Hispanics, and Moslems living in our country moved or were moved to the UPR along with leftists and atheists."

Kastenbaum nods. "You got lucky this time, Miss Braverman. I would suggest you not let your artistic daydreams get the better of you."

My nod is punctuated by the bell jolting everyone into action. Fortunately, tomorrow is a holiday, a welcome reprieve from this torture. Smiling to myself, I slide books and pens into my bag, grateful for the end of the school day.

"Hey," says Hannah as she waits for me to finish. "Holiday tomorrow." She nudges my shoulder.

I stand and lean closer so nobody else can hear. "Now that's what *I* call religious liberty," I whisper.

CHAPTER TWO

Dani

Columbus, North Ohio, United Progressive Regions

A boy! They fucking assigned me a boy when I'd asked to be matched up with a girl.

Shaking my head, I look away from the screen of my mom's ancient tablet. It's clear they did this on purpose because I'm queer. That had to be the reason. I can be in their precious pen pal program as long as it doesn't cause an international incident with the homophobic God Fearing States. More like the Garbage Fascist States.

I look back at the screen and click on the attachment mentioned in the email. Email of all things. Who still uses email?

Of course there it is, the first item.

Forbidden topics: homosexuality, gender identity disorders, atheism, socialism, communism, race relations, so-called women's rights, destruction of the unborn, so-called climate change, foreign relations, and any critiques of the GFS and its leaders that we deem to be derogatory. Any discussion of books and entertainment media forbidden by the GFS will be redacted from the correspondence and may result in the participant's dismissal from the program.

I close the attachment and let out a long sigh. What the hell is there left to talk about with this guy, Jeffrey Schwartz? You can only get so far with boring stuff like hobbies or school. Ugh, I hope he isn't some obnoxious jock or a military type itching to go serve in the Israeli army like so many Jewish GFS boys I've heard about from my brother. Well, there's no point in wondering. I'll just have to contact this Jeffrey Schwartz and find out for myself. Of course, that means signing up for an email address, something no one I know does anymore. Why bother when everyone is on their iBrains?

As I move my finger over the button to turn off the tablet, something occurs to me and I reread the message.

Dani Fine
431 Sojourner Terrace
Columbus, North Ohio UPR 5092
Sent via email to: meredith.schiller.fine@UPRmail.net

I look at my mom's email address which I'd used to submit the application, thinking I'd never get in anyway, even with my brother's connection. Binyamin asked, no, begged me to apply even though I was convinced I was not the kind of model Jewish teenager they were looking for. But I gave in out of curiosity, thinking this program would offer me a chance to learn about the GFS from someone my age who lives there.

But even after I sent the application, I figured they'd never take a queer kid whose father works for the UPR government and whose mother is our country's leading expert on climate change mitigation. So I was pretty shocked when about a half hour ago Mom triumphantly handed me her tablet.

"See, Ms. Pessimistic, you got in! I told you you would."

I roll my eyes and focus on the email from the Jewish Federation of North Ohio.

Dear Dani,

We are pleased to inform you that you have been selected to participate in the Cross-Border Dialogue Program for Jewish Teens. As you know, this is a pilot program designed to build bridges between Jewish teens living in the United Progressive Regions (UPR) and the God Fearing States (GFS). It is our hope that by encouraging youth in our two countries to get to know one another, we can strengthen the bonds between Jews. Greater understanding and empathy between the citizens of our two nations is one way we can help ensure the peaceful détente that our leaders have established remains in place for decades to come.

The word "détente" has been seared into our brains by teachers, content coaches, and online instructors. In school we are constantly reminded that there was never a war between the UPR and the GFS. That the former USA split because it became ungovernable. That we can live in peace with one another.

Ibi and Aisha think that's bullshit. You can't live in peace next to a bunch of racists and fundamentalists, they say. While there's a part of me that agrees, there's also a part that knows that my brother Binyamin, who chose to live in the GFS, is just an Orthodox Jew and not some fundamentalist hater. It's confusing, knowing that Binyamin, Miriam and their kids, all good people, are content to live in what everyone around me believes is a horrible place.

I sigh and go back to the email.

Your pen pal is Jeffrey Schwartz, a 17-year-old student at Kushner Academy for Boys in Cincinnati, South Ohio, GFS. While you and Jeffrey live in different countries–each with its own values, government, and culture—we believe you have a lot to learn from one another and may even discover you have much in common. Once you secure your own email address, you can communicate with Jeffrey by messaging him at jtech.schwartz@GFS.mail.net.

I stop reading and think about this Jeffrey Schwartz, hoping against hope that he's a decent human being like my brother. I continue and then come to the paragraph that gave me chills the first time I read it.

Please note that while you are free to discuss any subjects with

Jeffrey, we have been notified that GFS officials will randomly preview messages sent by and to their teens enrolled in the program. We therefore urge you to ensure that the contents of your communications conform to that country's standards for information sharing. While the Jewish Federation of North Ohio will not be previewing any messages, if the GFS determines that you have violated their guidelines, we will be forced to terminate you and your pen pal from the program.

It is our hope that if this pilot project is a success, we may one day be able to have our UPR-GFS "pen pals" meet in person. But that is a dream for another day.

I take a second look at Jeffrey's email address—Jtech. Schwartz. For a moment I let myself hope this guy is a techy nerd, maybe even a nonconformist. Is that even possible in the GFS? I grasp the edges of the tablet as the worst possibility becomes rooted into my brain. What if Jeffrey Schwartz is a homophobic racist misogynist?

My mother's voice comes barreling at me from the other side of the living room. "Dani, you ready to go?"

"Do I really have to?" I know I'm whining like a toddler.

My mother is a short woman, a trait I unfortunately inherited from her while my brother inherited my dad's above-average height. But amazingly my mom doesn't appear short. I don't know if it's how she carries herself with a no-nonsense posture that always seems to make her look like she's propelling herself forward with her long dark hair swept behind her like a superhero cape; or that serious look with her full lips pushed together into a straight line. Whatever it is, she never seems like she's actually just a fraction over five feet.

She's pulling on a red Windbreaker and motioning for me to get mine off the hook by the door. "Of course you have to go. We don't get many opportunities to see our region's federal executive in Columbus."

"Can I ask her why we had to get the only federal exec who's white?"

"You're not being fair to her. Josie's mother was almost killed in the assassinations that led to The Split. She's been a voice of reason in the government."

It's much too warm in October even for a Windbreaker,

so I decide not to listen to my mother. Since she's dragging me to this stupid event, I can at least make one little decision about it on my own. We walk out the front door and the house automatically locks up behind us. As we stand on the sidewalk waiting for our ride, I realize how annoyed I am by my mother's unconditional support for Josie Antonelli Clifford, one of four federal executives who run the UPR government, and the one assigned to our Midwest region. A lot of my friends think Josie only got elected because her mother, who was running for the USA Senate, was wounded in an assassination that killed both presidential candidates and ushered in The Split.

I decide to give my mother a little grief. "When you say Josie is the voice of reason, you really mean conservative, right?"

"Dani, just be grateful you didn't live in a time when you were surrounded by real conservatives. It's true, Josie is no radical, but there are a lot of people in this country, like me, who appreciate her progressive yet measured approach. If you want to hear about real conservatives, you can ask your new pen pal. What's his name again?"

"Jeffrey Schwartz. And how do I know he's not ultra conservative himself?"

"Well, I guess that's what this program is all about, getting to know one another."

"Except the GFS has so many restrictions on what we can talk about that I'm not gonna be able to say very much about myself."

"Come on, I know you," she says and puts her arm around me. "You'll find a way."

A blue AV pulls up in front of the house and we get in. As soon as our seat belts click, the car takes off.

"I'm glad you agreed to the AV, Mom."

"Only because you were so late getting ready. I would have preferred we ride our bikes. You know how I feel about cars and the environment, even these driverless rideshares."

The AV, which has three rows for its passengers, makes two more stops after we cross the river. It's more than likely the presence of other people keeps my mother from commenting in that exasperated tone of voice she has that the trip would have been faster if we'd biked.

The other people in the AV are also quiet except for an older white woman with gray hair piled on top of her head and what might be her dark-skinned, curly-haired grandson. He's singing the alphabet song and she's trying to keep his voice soft, but he shouts out the letter P and then breaks into giggles. I smile at them and feel a familiar pang in my stomach that I have never had the chance to meet my brother's young children. Sadness morphs into anger as I silently curse the GFS for depriving me of watching my niece and nephews grow up and I picture in my mind the paragraph in the email listing the long list of topics that I can't discuss with my pen pal.

The car stops to let us off on North High Street instead of pulling into the roadway adjacent to the auditorium. Everyone on our ride gets out, and as I take my first look at the crowd outside Mershon Auditorium, I see that the campus roads in this area have been blocked off with metal barriers. It's a mob scene with demonstrators shouting and holding a sea of neon signs above their heads.

"Josie, Let Them In!" is both a chant and a popular sign protesting the government's decision not to immediately house and settle the thousands of climate refugees who are coming from island nations that have been inundated by the rising seas and from countries whose farm lands have turned to desert.

There's also a crowd of people promoting various ideas for the renaming of the city of Columbus, which will soon no longer honor a genocidal imperialist.

I'm surprised to be offered flyers by some of the demonstrators because its common knowledge that the production of paper is a leading cause of deforestation. But I'm curious, so I agree to take a few. One favors renaming the city Shawnee for the tribe whose land we stole. Another wants us to choose Owens for the athlete Jesse Owens, who was born in Columbus. There's Granville for the African American inventor, Granville Woods, also from Columbus. And when I look up, I see a bunch of signs with names like Obama, Mandela, Chavez, and the name Phil Ochs, who my mother tells me was a folk singer.

I toss the papers in a recycling shredder outside the auditorium. My mother, a member of the city assembly, is supporting Shawnee, though there's already a village in Ohio with that name.

"So we'll be New Shawnee," she says. "I like the idea of honoring the Indigenous. It's the least we can do."

In the lobby my mother and I are directed to a section of the auditorium reserved for city assembly members. On the way to our seats I see Trey and Julia, my two best friends, sitting on the aisle in the back row. They are holding hands because they are cutest couple ever. I nudge Trey's arm and say hi.

"Is Aisha here?" I ask them, wondering if my very radical girlfriend would even be interested in listening to Josie.

The two of them look at one another like they are trying to figure out what to tell me. That's enough of a clue to make me realize something's up.

"Who's she with?" I ask.

"Mostly with the Let Them In folks," says Julia, "but I think she might also be hanging with the Emmas."

I nod. The Emma Goldman Anarchist Cell is Aisha's activist group. When I hear my mother sigh at the mention of the Emmas, I tell Julia and Trey to wait for me in the lobby afterward. It's time to get going before my mom and I end up in our usual political argument about anarchist tactics. Besides, the hologram timer just flashed in front of us beginning the two-minute countdown, so I guess The Josie Show is about to begin.

Sinking down in my seat, I'm determined to only half-listen. Josie is introduced by Shel Chasen, one of our senators, who came out as Enby recently. Shel is an actual Shawnee and starts every speech with an invocation to their ancestors. We stand up for this and my mother whispers, "You see why we need to rename the city for the Shawnee?"

I tune out most of Shel's introduction of Josie, but my mother pulls me up by the arm to stand again when our esteemed federal executive walks onto the stage. I'm sure this is about saving face so that the other city assembly members won't start gossiping about Meredith Schiller-Fine's radical daughter.

Josie walks across the stage during the applause, waving and pointing to people like the politician she is. As soon as we're seated and quiet, the chanting of "Let Them In" from the upper level begins. I hear people in the rows behind me join in. Josie stands silent and waits.

She's not bad looking for a woman over forty. Kind of short with dark, layered hair that reaches her shoulders. She has that classically Italian prominent nose that doesn't dominate her face but instead lends it an air of seriousness. I wonder what she looked like when she was a teenager and if I'd have found her attractive.

Throughout the speech my mother can't stop herself from sharing her opinions, even though I'm trying so hard to tune it all out. When Josie mentions something about balancing the need to admit refugees with our own need to protect the environment and avoid overcrowding, my mother again pulls me by the arm so she can whisper in my ear. "That's the right approach if we all don't want to wind up as refugees."

I do have to hand it to Josie. She doesn't shy away from controversy. Not only is she talking to the Let Them In folks, she's explaining why she has "important concerns" about our country's boycott of Israel, which the UPR began after the Israeli government annexed all of the Palestinian territories.

My brother Binyamin was on the very last teen tour of UPR kids allowed to travel to Israel. After that, there were sanctions and a boycott. We don't even have an embassy there anymore, just a small office with the actual embassy in Ramallah. A lot of that makes sense to me. A country that occupies a people is operating way outside the UN Declaration of Human Rights that the UPR has adopted.

As Josie continues to explain her position on Israel, my mother nods in agreement.

"I can't believe you oppose the boycott," I tell her.

She turns to me and whispers her usual response when the subject comes up. "You haven't been there. I have."

Finally, Josie ends the speech with her support for our decision to get rid of the Columbus name. As the applause, cheering and booing begin, I bolt from my mother so I can go find Julia and Trey.

Luckily they are both tall and I easily spot them in a corner of the lobby standing aside from the crowd streaming outside.

"Let's see if we can find Aisha," I tell them.

They both look at one another and then anywhere but right at me. "Uh Dani," says Trey, "that may not be a good idea right now."

"Why not?" And then I realize in an instant why not. Aisha must be out there with her arm around some other girl, a sight I definitely don't want to see. Even though I have reluctantly agreed to her demand for an open relationship, it was not my first choice.

"I get it," I tell them and decide it's time for a change of subject. "How about we go somewhere and hang out and I can tell you all about my GFS pen pal."

"You got in?" asks Trey, incredulous.

"By some miracle, yeah, I did."

CHAPTER THREE

Judith

I'll never admit it to anyone, but I don't love Shabbat, the Jewish Sabbath. As a child, I tagged along with my mother as we spent Thursday afternoons and evenings rushing from the kosher butcher to the green grocer to the fish man, wedged into the crowds of women with strollers, carriages, and shopping carts, yelling out their orders, waving their arms to get attention, their fists clutching red and green GFS dollars.

When I was older and started attending Kushner Academy for Girls, the whole school was dismissed at two p.m. on Fridays so we could help our mothers prepare for the Sabbath. Even though I'm not a big fan of Kushner Academy, I'd rather stay at school instead of being thrust into the weekly whirlwind of preparation for Shabbat: cleaning the bedroom I share with my sister, scrubbing the bathtub, vacuuming, polishing the silver.

The only bright spot occurs every third week when it's my turn to make the challah, the one chore that requires some artistic talent. I take as much time as I can inventing complex braids for the thick strands of dough I knead, trying to make each loaf more beautiful than the last one I made. Without fail, my sisters accuse me of dragging my feet so I can avoid chopping carrots and onions for the chicken soup or slicing apples and pears for the fruit compote. But I do my best to ignore them, focusing instead on how eight lengths of dough can be twisted into a masterpiece.

Inevitably I feel my mother tap my shoulder and I'm confronted with *the look*. Her head tilted to the side, her brow furrowed. I get her unspoken message. *Enough already with the challah, there's a lot of other work for you.*

I usually spend Shabbat morning in synagogue, sitting with Hannah who lifts her prayer book to cover our mouths so we won't be caught whispering. We walk home at a leisurely pace, talking about whatever boy Hannah has set her sights on and whatever papercut design I'm working on.

On most Saturday nights, once Shabbat ends, I can resume what I think of as my normal life. There's an old wooden table in the basement of our house that I've been able to claim as my art desk. Long ago, when I was in kindergarten, a papercut artist came to our school. She told us a story about Rabbi Shem Tov who lived in the 1400s. He was writing a book when his inkwell froze solid, so he continued to write by cutting the letters out of paper with a knife. From that day on I was entranced by the idea that words and pictures could be created by cutting paper. While most of my papercuts look like something everyone would recognize, like a scene from the Torah or the words of a psalm, I still think of papercutting as an almost secretive art form. Every now and then I figure out a way to include little coded messages in the background of a picture, just to prove that I can. It's fun and something I share only with Hannah.

Hannah also is the only one who knows about my gift of seeing *neshamah*. And even though she says that you don't need a gift to know that Yetta Freundlich has no soul, she is always eager to hear about other people who have revealed themselves to me.

Today after synagogue, the afternoon drags on. I read for a while and take a nap, but I'm restless, my hands itching to grab hold of a pencil or a pair of scissors, both forbidden on Shabbat.

While I normally retreat to my art desk after Shabbat ends, tonight is different. I'm not able to look forward to a few hours of quiet creativity. Instead, as the sun sinks lower into the sky, I am dressing to go out, my mother and older sister hovering.

"Yes, I think that navy skirt looks good. It has a nice line. What do you think, Shuli?"

My sister nods and hums her agreement. "It'll go well with the white blouse, the one with the navy buttons."

I feel like a mannequin, something in the center of the action but ignored.

When my younger sister calls out from another room, my mother goes running. I can feel my body loosening up, the tension in my shoulders gone as soon as my mother leaves the room. I love her and there's ways in which we are not at all different. We both love Hashem and try to obey His commandments. We are homebodies who feel most comfortable in our small domains. We even look alike; both short with soft round bodies and dark curly hair. Mine reaches right below my shoulders while my mother's is above hers usually covered by a *tichel*, the scarf that all married Orthodox women in our community wear.

Even with our similarities I am always feeling at odds with my mother. She loves my papercuts and she oohs and ahhs over the finished product, but she frowns upon all the time I spend at my art table working on them. She is always reminding me that once Shuli is married I will be next. When she says that I give her a weak smile because I cannot feel any of the joy that comes through in her words.

Shuli places her hands on my shoulders. "Your first mixer. Are you excited? Nervous?"

I'm not sure either describes my feelings. Mostly I've been hoping to suddenly come down with some dread disease like last year when I was bedridden with the flu.

"I-I don't know."

Shuli squeezes my shoulders. "It'll be fine. Look how it worked out for me. I met David there two years ago when we were your age and now we're getting married in a few months. I pray the same thing can happen for you."

I force a smile and a little nod, grateful that it's enough to satisfy my sister. When she turns to walk a few steps back, she doesn't hear what I whisper as quietly as possible. "Please Hashem, don't answer Shuli's prayer."

* * *

I'd been to the boys' academy before when my brother was younger and had to be walked to school. It's around the corner from the girls' academy. Their building is bigger than my school's, mostly to accommodate the large gymnasium and the ball fields. The girls' academy has a small gym in the basement where we learn gymnastics and Israeli dances.

Hannah is waiting by the entrance, shifting from one foot to the other, a habit I know means she's either nervous, excited, or both. She's been talking about this mixer for the past month, hoping she'll be able to have the opportunity to talk to Isaac, Rabbi Leventhal's son. He's in our grade at the boys' school, and Hannah has been eyeing him at synagogue begging me to take a hard look at his soul. Luckily, when I did it shimmered, which only made Hannah more determined.

Like all the girls, Hannah is dressed modestly. But unlike the other girls she stands out. Her long light brown wavy hair falls down her back and her green eyes are striking. She's wearing a long-sleeved blouse and a skirt that covers her knees. She has been planning this outfit for the past week. The skirt she'd described endlessly is a burnt orange that goes perfectly with the off-white blouse, which is embroidered on the neckline with burnt orange thread. As soon as I see her in that outfit, I know Hannah will have no trouble attracting the attention of Isaac Leventhal or any other boy. Even I can't help a sharp intake of breath when I first notice her.

The gym is decorated in blue and white, the colors of the Israeli flag. Crepe paper streamers hang from the ceiling and there are small bouquets of blue and white balloons on the round tables set up along the back wall.

Hannah went to last year's mixer and recounted the event to me once I recovered from the flu. So this year she helps me understand exactly how this whole event works.

"We start out separated. The boys sit on this side and we're over here," she says as she points to the tables on the right side of the room. "Later it gets more interesting."

We head to an empty table, avoiding the one where Yetta sits holding court with a group of our classmates.

Both schools call this a mixer and not a dance because we are forbidden to dance with one another until we're married. Instead, teachers and administrators organize some getting-to-know-you games that don't involve touching, and then encourage us to sit together over refreshments and talk.

Luckily for me, participating in the games is voluntary, and I plan to sit them out while Hannah tells me she's going right over to the front row of chairs set up in the middle of the room so Isaac will notice her. I wish her luck before we separate and am relieved when she doesn't push me to join in.

I sit alone at the table and watch as the boys are asked a series of questions and told to raise their hands to respond.

"Which of you has traveled to Israel?" Almost every hand is raised.

"Which of you is planning to enlist in the Israeli army?" About ten hands go up. Luckily Isaac's isn't one of them.

"How many of your families relocated to the GFS during the Great Migration?" I can't help but feel my shoulders tense with annoyance when the years after The Split are referred to with the term that belongs to another era and to another people. But I still take note of the fact that about half of the boys raise their hands. Again, Isaac's stays down.

When the questioning switches to the girls, my attention wanders since the only reason I watched any of it was to support Hannah in her quest to get to know Isaac. I head over to the long table with the refreshments just so it looks like I'm doing something other than sitting by myself like the misfit I am. There are pitchers of water, some kind of grape juice, and a platter with cookies, each topped by a button of chocolate in the center. I recognize them from the neighborhood bakery.

As I lean forward to take a paper cup off the top of a stack, I notice a boy sitting in a chair against the wall at the far end of the table. His head is bent over a book, enabling me to see his navy blue yarmulke with small flecks of silver on it. It reminds me of the night sky. I watch as he turns the page of a book covered in brown paper. What could he be reading?

Right at that moment a blinding light radiates from the boy, its shimmer pulsing for what feels like at least ten seconds. In shock I jump a half-step back, nearly tripping over my feet. I've never before fixed on such a *neshamah*. Isaac Leventhal's had been more like a pleasant sparkle that flashed for a few seconds and then dimmed. My brother Morty's was the same. Hannah's was brighter, but nothing like this.

I have no idea how to approach a boy, but I know I need to know this one.

"I like your yarmulke. It reminds me of the planetarium."

He glances up and mumbles a "Thanks" that sounds more like a groan and goes back to his book. He's probably shy. When he'd looked up for a few seconds, I noticed straight light brown hair, a roundish face and a pug nose.

"What are you reading?"

"A book." He's not shy, he's annoyed.

"Can I see?"

He sighs audibly, holds his place in the book with a finger and opens to the title page.

The Soul of a New Machine by Tracy Kidder.

"I don't know that book. Is it new? What kind of a machine is it about?"

His head is back in the book again as he speaks in a staccato rhythm.

"No. Nineteen eighty-one. Computers."

I wonder why he's reading such an old book, since anything written about computers back then would be obsolete by now. But asking about his book seems to be getting me nowhere. Instead I carry over a chair and sit down next to him. He raises his head, sits back in his chair and lets out a quick blast of breath. I take advantage of the opportunity to open a new topic.

"I'm not very happy about being here. I'm guessing you feel the same."

He closes his eyes and shakes his head. "Your powers of deduction are astounding."

I don't react, thinking it best to just ignore his sarcasm. I'm determined to get to know him. I just can't walk away from a soul that blasted toward me like a comet, leaving me in awe and a bit unsettled. I try again.

"I'm Judith Braverman and I'd rather be home working on a papercut for Sukkot."

He looks up and rolls his eyes at me. "Good for you Judith Braverman. Getting a big jump on the holiday that's a month away. Are you in some kind of a competition to be crowned Super Jew?"

Despite his attempt to drive me away, I feel neither insulted nor angry. If anything, his surly attitude intrigues me. While I haven't spoken to many boys my age, the few I've met were polite and shy, not aggressive and cynical like this one. Maybe he needs to hear what he sounds like.

"Do you have a name, Planetarium Boy?"

Finally, a smile—lopsided with one side of his mouth pushed up, followed by another round of head shaking.

"Jeffrey Schwartz, chief curmudgeon at your service, Miss Braverman, Super Jew. What brings you to my little corner of paradise?"

I hesitate. I don't want him to think my interest in him is romantic. But should I tell him the truth, that the blast of light from his soul nearly knocked me to the floor? I decide to take a chance and then if it doesn't go well, convince him that I'm joking.

"You see, um, there's this thing I can do. It doesn't work for everyone and I'm not sure why it works for some people and not for others. But it, uh, worked for you."

Jeffrey leans back in his chair, the book still open on his lap. "A thing, huh?" His chest shakes with laughter.

I take a deep breath, my shoulders raised, and brace myself. "I can see your *neshamah*, your soul. Usually, when the *neshamah* is a good one, there's a little shimmer. But in your case…"

"There's a black hole, right?" Jeffrey is leaning forward, his chin resting in the palm of his hand. He smiles.

I raise my hands signaling him to stop. "No! No! It was a blinding light that almost threw me off my feet. I've never seen one like that before. So I, um, wanted to meet you."

He stares at me, his mouth closed, the smile gone. "You are one interesting Super Jew, Miss Braverman. You make me almost want to believe you."

My voice is almost a whisper. "It's all true."

"So this isn't some elaborate yet misguided pickup line?" His voice takes on a higher register. "Oh, Jeffrey, your *neshamah* is so big and shiny."

"No, I promise," I say through my laughter.

Jeffrey dips his head and points up to the yarmulke. "Well then, we'll have to chalk it up to the stars on this little planetarium up here. Because believe me, there's no way I'm some great soul man."

But I think he is. And in the depths of my own soul I know it.

CHAPTER FOUR

Dani

Now that I have an email address, I can stop using my mom's tablet (a fitting name since it's about as old as the tablets that have the Ten Commandments etched into them). Instead I fit my small black iBrain onto the side of my head and begin to speak to Kat, my personal bot. I named her myself because I've always wanted a friend named Kat and because I wanted to honor Anne Frank, who named her diary Kitty.

"Kat, open my new email account and send a message to Jeffrey Schwartz."

I let out a sigh of exasperation. This is so clunky! The newest version of iBrain allows you to just silently dictate the letter by thinking it "brain to iBrain" as the ads say. Aisha showed me hers and I'm soooo jealous.

"Ready when you are," Kat's silky voice responds inside my head. Once again I shiver a bit when that mellifluous voice I chose for her comes through.

"Hey Jeffrey," I begin. "Sorry it took a while to write. I actually had to get an email address since the pen pal program requires it. Kinda lame, if you ask me, when we can have a perfectly good conversation using iBrains, but hey, sometimes ya gotta go with the program, right? Okay, so I have a million questions for you, such as..."

Wait. Should I tell him something about myself before I interrogate him? I have Kat read me back what I'd said.

"Kat, take out that last part and instead say, "But I'll start with stuff about me. I'm seventeen, in the eleventh grade at James Baldwin High School in Columbus, which, by the way, might not be called Columbus too much longer because of the obvious associations (I'll let you know when there's a change). I joined the pen pal program because I'm curious about people who live in other countries. I know a little bit about the GFS because my brother lives there. He's a professor at U...

"Kat, take out the 'professor' sentence and replace it with, "You see, he went to Israel when he was a teenager and became pretty religious and also met this girl (his wife now) and she was also pretty religious. So he relocated to Cincinnati, but he's able to come up here to visit a few times a year, and that's why I know a bit about your country and your city."

Is this too much information or will it make Jeffrey more comfortable knowing I have a religious brother who lives in the GFS? I decide to go with him being more comfortable.

"Anyway, what I really want to do one day is become a visi-tech for something like International Geographic. Or maybe an anthropologist and use visuals for something meaningful while still getting to travel around the world.

"It's not that things aren't okay here in the UPR. I'm in charge of streaming media for the school news site and have recently been playing with holograms. They are so cool! I hang out with my friends who also work on the site and are part of my project group, but...I don't know. I guess I'm kind of restless and curious. I can't help but think there's something I still need to discover.

"So I want to know everything about you, starting with your email address. Are you a techie kinda guy? That would be cool since I use a lot of tech tools and stuff and was hoping I got matched up with someone who was into that.

"Okay, a million other things, but I'll wait to hear from you.

"Bye for now, Dani."

* * *

"Hey Twenty-Five, c'mere. I wanna show you the layout for your visuals this week."

Ibi calls to me across the room where I sit with Aisha whispering in heated tones about our relationship, or what feels like our non-relationship lately. Ibi is intent on sticking with that ridiculous nickname that's meant to broadcast to the world that I'm one-quarter African American. My friends think it's hysterical, some kind of twisted satire of the Jim Crow era when a drop of Black blood would disqualify someone from being treated as white.

I'm proud that my grandfather on my mom's side is African American and I'm not all that comfortable with my racial heritage being treated as some kind of joke.

But Ibi, Aisha, Trey, and Julia have all bought into this and I try to be a good sport since they're my closest friends. Though in the case of Aisha, she's something more than just a friend, except the way things are going with us, I'm not even sure if we will end up liking each other.

"Dani," she says as she leans over the table where we sit opposite one another, "I don't see how anything would be different were I to agree to be exclusive with you." She's talking to me in what we all call her "royal voice."

Since no one is immune from Ibi's habit of affixing nicknames, he has dubbed Aisha "the Gullah Princess," a reference to her auspicious heritage as a descendent of the Gullah-Geechee nation and the granddaughter of one of the founders of Black Lives Matter a few years before The Split. I know for a fact that she's both proud of this legacy and terrified to death that she'll never live up to it. People are always coming over to her like she's somebody famous. It gets a bit exhausting after a while.

I look down at the table, staring at the white surface and mumble, "I just know I would feel different if I wasn't worried all the time that you were with someone else."

She sits back shaking her head, arms crossed over her chest, her long, thin braids resting on them. A groan escapes her. "This is getting us nowhere."

It's not an argument I'm gonna win and I know it. Aisha and I have been having this same fight for weeks. When she first brought up the topic of polyamory, I grudgingly went along with it. At that point we'd only stepped over the line from friends to girlfriends for about a month.

When I asked Trey and Julia what they thought, they told me I was crazy to agree to this since I am too neurotic to be in anything but a monogamous relationship.

"You can't even deal with me liking someone else's visuals," Julia said, rolling her eyes. "How are you gonna deal with Aisha dating other people? You'll be a wreck."

She totally called it. It was almost a certainty that on the first Friday night that Aisha would tell me she was "busy," I'd be lying in bed at home shaking with jealousy, convinced there was someone else with their hands all over her, rolling their tongue inside her mouth.

"Twenty-Five." That's Ibi again. "Can you tear yourself away from the irresistible Gullah Princess for one minute and come look at these visis?"

Aisha makes a motion with her head in Ibi's direction. Clearly, the Princess is dismissing me.

I stand with a sigh and take a few steps in Ibi's direction. Then turn back, eager to have the last word.

"To be continued later," I say loud enough so she can hear me. She doesn't look in my direction and her shoulders lift in a shrug.

CHAPTER FIVE

Jeffrey

There's very little that interests me at school. Really, it's just a boring, propaganda-filled indoctrination program. Not just the Judaism, but all the rah-rah about the GFS and the trashing of the UPR. That's why I signed up for the pen pal program. I wanted to learn more about a place where it might be possible for me to really live free.

It's not that I hate being Jewish. I mean, it's okay. The food is pretty amazing and, uhhh, we are the Chosen People. Though these days it feels like we've been chosen for getting beat up and having our synagogues defaced with swastikas. Thanks a lot for choosing us, God.

I take my seat in history class behind Isaac Leventhal, the rabbi's son. We aren't exactly close friends, but unlike most of these so-called pious students, Leventhal doesn't harass me. The only other guys that treat me okay are the members of the Tech Team. Everyone else here either ignores me (for which, believe me, I'm grateful) or gives me a hard time about, well, everything.

First off, I get a lot of grief about my height and boyish appearance. "Schwartz, when you gonna reach puberty? That beard's never gonna come in."

Then they criticize my cynical attitude. "Schwartz, not everything is a waste of your time. When exactly did your time become more valuable than all of ours?"

Oh, and when they really want to go for the jugular, they make fun of my total disinterest in girls. "Schwartz-y, you're not gonna catch anything from them, you know. Don't make everyone think you're a *fagele*."

That last one is particularly worrisome because the truth is, I'm gay, I am a *fagele*. I have no interest in girls. And when Isaac Leventhal smiles at me because he's just a good guy who doesn't give me shit, my stomach flip-flops. Not that I would ever tell him or anyone else.

Maybe that's why I decided to become friends with Judith Braverman, Super Jew and reader of souls. She's a girl, so they can all back off on the *fagele* stuff, and, more importantly, she doesn't look at me the way I see girls looking at my classmates. Like all gooey and stuff. Instead she kids around with me, calling me Planetarium Boy and telling me funny stories about the souls she's claimed to see. It doesn't make me tense to be around her, worried that she's expecting something from me that I can't deliver. Instead it just feels relaxed and comfortable.

"Gentlemen, please come to attention." Our history teacher raises his hands like he's starting to conduct an orchestra. "We are fortunate to have a very special guest who'll be speaking to us today on the history of antisemitism."

Oh gee, a special guest. Let's hope he's more exciting than old man Peltz whose voice has no ability to do anything but drip out in a monotone. Anyone with insomnia only has to spend fifteen minutes in this guy's lecture and they'll be cured. I look at the man standing next to Peltz. He's tall. Okay, everyone is taller than my teacher, and me, I suppose. His dark beard is trimmed, not long and bushy, and he has a kind of flat nose. I'm too far back to see his eye color, but I notice that he squints when he smiles, which is kind of cute.

"This is Professor Binyamin Fine from the University of Cincinnati, an expert in antisemitism. He'll be speaking to you about the years leading up to the Shoah in both Europe and the former United States of America."

As he's being introduced, Professor Fine turns his back to us and writes his name on the blackboard. F-I-N-E—spelled the same way as my pen pal's. Could he be Dani's brother who lives here in Cincinnati? Although we've only exchanged a few emails so far, I'm eager to know more about her. Could I be lucky enough to actually meet someone in her family?

It's been a whole week since her last email and I haven't written back. Now that we've shared all the surface stuff about ourselves, I'm just not sure what more to say about my life here that wouldn't get me kicked out of the program. Mostly I just want to learn about the UPR from someone who actually lives there. Why is her city looking to change its name? What's the problem with Columbus that she was so sure I'd understand?

As Professor Fine calls the class to order, I put these questions aside, hoping that our cute guest speaker has something worthwhile to say.

It turns out he does. I sit through the lecture in rapt attention as Professor Fine takes us through the spread of antisemitism in the pre-Nazi Weimar Republic and then into the 1930s, with Kristallnacht—the Night of Broken Glass—the culminating event. Jewish stores looted. Synagogues burned. People dragged out of their homes and murdered. All while the police stood by and did nothing.

He pauses and looks at each of us. His gaze is intense and I wonder if my classmates feel it the way I do. The unsaid words coming from him penetrate my brain: *Are you paying attention? Can you see what's right in front of you today?*

Instead he ends this part of his lecture with just one question. "What would you have done?"

I feel my heartbeat quicken and my breath leave me. I squirm in my seat. But I don't look away.

His lecture on the United States of America is thankfully less violent, but his warning is just as chilling.

"True, there was no equivalent to Kristallnacht, even when thousands of pro-Nazi Americans filled Madison Square Garden in New York for their own hate rally. And it was only when the attack on Pearl Harbor in 1941 catapulted the USA into war that the antisemitism of the Henry Fords and the Bishop Coughlins were silenced. Then for a while, beginning in the 1960s, things began to look up. Anti-Jewish quotas at universities were lifted. Restrictive covenants in real estate developments were outlawed. Jews were successful in a wide range of professions.

"But let me leave you with one final question, gentlemen, something you can ponder together or on your own. Looking back at our history and reflecting on our lives in a new country that guarantees us religious freedom and the right to emigrate to Israel, are we really at last safe?"

I sit trembling at my desk. My heart racing and my breathing labored. Professor Fine is the first person who has given voice to what I've been seeing around me that no one else wants to acknowledge. Here, in the (Supposed) God Fearing States, in the city of Cincinnati, antisemitism has once again taken hold. Not in the form of a major conflagration like Kristallnacht, instead more like dozens of small brush fires easily stamped out and forgotten, but still continuing with no end in sight. And what will happen when some of those brush fires connect to one another and begin to burn across our neighborhoods? Will it then be too late?

"Mr. Schwartz, don't you have another class?"

Peltz's voice rouses me to the realization that I am the only one still sitting in the class. Everyone else has left except for my teacher and Professor Fine, both of them looking right at me.

"I-I wanted to ask Professor Fine something, if that's okay?" My voice is shaking. I lift my body from the desk seat with great difficulty.

He walks toward me, his forehead crinkled in concern. His voice is soft. "Of course."

I lay my hands flat against the wooden desk, worried that I'll otherwise be unable to hold myself up. Professor Fine nods his head slightly, encouraging me to continue.

Suddenly I feel foolish, knowing he's expecting some kind of question about his lecture. I could easily meet that expectation and ask him if he really thinks we Jews are in trouble today. But somehow what I want to ask him looms larger in my mind, even though it might seem trivial to him.

"Is…is…uh…" I hesitate and then force myself to just get the words out. "Is Dani Fine your sister?"

His eyes are wide and his mouth opens though he says nothing for a few seconds.

"How would you know that?" I hear caution in his voice and maybe a little worry.

At least I can put his mind at ease. "I'm her pen pal, you know, through the Federation."

His smile is wide and I hear him exhale audibly. "Yes, Dani's my sister."

He steps closer to me with his hand out. I shake it. "I'm Jeffrey." My voice is at last normal.

Peltz nods, having heard. "What are the chances?" he says and looks upward. "*Baruch Hashem*. He works His magic once again."

Indeed, *Baruch Hashem*, blessed is God. At least now I know what I can write about when I email Dani.

CHAPTER SIX

Judith

Jeffrey is my first male friend. "Not a boyfriend," I keep reminding Hannah, who just nods to go along with me but constantly makes it clear that she still believes otherwise. As Isaac Leventhal has begun to show an interest in her, she's become invested in me being with Jeffrey as if there's some kind of natural symmetry that must be achieved.

As for me, I'm content to demonstrate symmetry with my papercuts. The logic of it has always been the attraction. If you cut into a folded sheet of paper, you can be sure you'll create two identical shapes that mirror one another, each on its own side of the divide. There's comfort in that, and beauty as well.

On Saturdays, Jeffrey and I are able to meet up during the Kiddish lunch after Shabbat services. A few times a week, at the end of the school day, he walks around the corner and finds me lingering with Hannah on the outside steps of Kushner Academy for Girls. When she sees him, Hannah waves, a big smile on her face, and makes a forward motion with her hands, urging me toward him. I sigh at her with resignation, but the truth is I'm glad to see him.

These meetings have spread news of our friendship throughout my school, along with speculation about whether we're a couple. Yetta, that malevolent creature who sees herself as the self-appointed enforcer of purity, watches us especially closely. She stands nearby and stares as we walk together, hoping to notice if we'll slip and touch, something that's forbidden. But we're careful and we never give her the satisfaction.

Today, once I'm dismissed by Hannah, and Jeffrey and I take a few steps in the direction of my house, he suddenly stops and turns around to stare back at Yetta. "What's your problem?" he calls out in a loud, angry voice.

It all happens so fast that I don't have a second to stop him. I wish I could have. Hannah and I have agreed for some time that the best way to disarm Yetta is to ignore her. But that's obviously not how Jeffrey sees it; and I have to admit that a part of me is glad he said something. No one ever challenges Yetta, so it's exciting when at last somebody does. It seems even she is surprised since she just stands there staring at him, her eyes wide open and one arm out with a finger pointing at him. Jeffrey and I turn away from her and start walking.

Jeffrey brings out a side of me I mostly keep hidden except at times with Hannah. His cynicism about school, our community, and our country awaken my own doubts and concerns. It's not that I question my faith as a Jew. In that I am resolute. But I do wonder if all the other trappings ("great word," Jeffrey says when I use it) are necessary. Like the push to get married and the need to remain in our insulated neighborhood when we become adults. Jeffrey makes me wonder what the wider world could offer me.

He's in that pen pal program with the UPR and has told me about Dani, the girl who wrote to him about her iBrain and how she doesn't have to go to school every day but only once every two weeks. She's told him that most of her classes are virtual, except for when she meets with her project team, whatever that is.

"She's kind of an artist like you, SJ. She's into something she calls visuals and wants to travel around the world. Also, she's Jewish but not at all religious."

Jewish but not religious? What could that even mean? And the desire to travel around the world? What an enormous dream. And how unrealistic for a girl. Won't her family be wanting her to get married?

It's not that I'm not curious about places outside of Cincinnati, but I'm happy just making my papercuts at home, at my little desk in the basement, not like this girl who's been given a boy's name and has such big ambitions.

Today, as we continue this conversation about his strange pen pal, that blinding white and silver light from Jeffrey's soul blasts toward me, forcing me to stop walking and shut my eyes.

He laughs as he watches me reel back. "Ah, SJ, gotta watch out for that killer soul of mine."

I smile back at him but I don't really find any of this funny. Instead, it's a big mystery. Why do I experience his soul this way when that doesn't happen with anyone else? I've spent many nights in bed and Saturday mornings in shul praying to Hashem for an answer.

The books that might explain this, the ones about Jewish mysticism and the Kaballah, are restricted in the school library so I can't get access to them. As we stand in front of my house to say goodbye, I think of asking Jeffrey if he can figure out a way to get those books for me. Maybe they aren't forbidden for the boys. But I worry he'll just laugh at me since he thinks the whole "soul thing" as he called it is just a joke.

* * *

I am turning this problem over in my head at breakfast the next morning as my mother slides a plate of scrambled eggs and toast in front of me.

My father's loud voice breaks through my thoughts, preceding his entry into the kitchen. "This week's edition, hot off the press!"

It's clear to all of us from the big smile on his face and the twinkle in his eye that he's just come from an early morning trip to the printer's and has copies of this week's *Jewish Community News* tucked under his arm and resting against his bulky frame. The paper is his pride and joy, likely more so than the pride he takes in his four children.

"Thank you," I say as he lays a copy on the table next to my plate. He gives me a quick peck on the cheek, and I feel the bristles of his dark brown beard on my skin.

I unfold the large paper and scan the front page. Coverage of the High Holidays takes up the most space, and there's a small area at the bottom dedicated to an article about the elderly Rabbi Yacov Kuriel, who's become quite ill and is feared to be at death's door. I skim the first few paragraphs about the seriousness of his condition and then open the paper to the page where the story is continued. There's a photo of the rabbi in his younger days, still with a long beard, beginning to turn gray, and small intense eyes, the color uncertain in the black and white photograph. He was quite thin even back then, but the intensity of his gaze cannot be disputed. I wish I could get a fix on his soul, but I know from experience that isn't possible with just a photograph. I'd have to see him in person.

And then an idea comes to me. I read the rest of the article carefully to confirm what I'm thinking. Yes, there it is. Rabbi Kuriel is revered as a mystic, someone who has studied Kaballah with elderly masters in Israel and whose insights about the course of world events have proven true time and again. He'd foretold The Split of the USA and was one of the leading rabbis who urged pious Jews to stay together in the GFS. Once The Split occurred, the accuracy of his prediction made him practically a legend and he was sought out for advice and counsel by Jews from all over.

The article convinces me that Rabbi Kuriel could explain my gift of seeing into souls and why it only works on some people. And just maybe he could explain my strong reaction when I see Jeffrey's soul. But Rabbi Kuriel is near death, so I'll have to move quickly.

"Sad about old Rabbi Kuriel, huh?" My father's voice comes from behind me. He's reading over my shoulder.

I put the paper down. "Do you know if he's receiving guests?" I ask. And quickly add, "I thought maybe I could bring him something or create a papercut with a prayer for his healing, like the *Mi Shebarach*."

My question was out before I even thought about it. Luckily I had the presence of mind to cloak my desire to see the rabbi in the guise of a sick call, adding the last part to make my father think I would be using my art as a kind of get well card.

My mother smiles and nods. "That's a lovely thought, Judith." But she doesn't give me permission to go ahead with this idea because she knows that final approval will have to come from my father.

"You can try," he says, his tone doubtful. "He may be too ill for visitors, but you can leave the papercut with his daughter, Dvorah. She's the one taking care of him."

* * *

The house is ordinary, not the palace I'd imagined for such an important man. There are two levels, with an expanse of neatly trimmed lawn in the front and a row of short bushes along the walkway.

I'm dressed even more modestly than usual, not wanting to distract Rabbi Kuriel by offending him with my appearance. It's hot today, in the nineties, normal for late October, but I'm wearing a long-sleeved, light green blouse with a pink cardigan. My forest green skirt is two inches below my knees and my legs are covered in tights. I've tied my curly black hair back from my face, hoping at least that would give me some relief from the heat. I can feel the sweat I've worked up walking here rolling down my back. I'm hoping the house is air-conditioned.

I have the papercut in a folder in my bag. I'd spent hours on it the last few nights, carving out the Hebrew letters and deciding which parts of the prayer I wanted to use. I've set the prayer in the center of the Tree of Life, which I thought was a fitting symbol. I used a bluish-green paper for the tree and the prayer and set them against an ivory background, light enough for contrast but not white, which is the color of death.

My mother gasped in amazement when I showed it to her. "Magnificent! *Baruch Hashem*, you have such a gift, Judith. This is worthy of a man like Rabbi Kuriel."

I was relieved at her reaction and also a little amused. I've never told my mother about my other gift, the one that lets me see into souls. If I told her, she'd definitely tell my father and that would lead to a trip to Rabbi Leventhal and maybe even a psychiatrist. I worry that they'd think I was suffering from delusions and link that somehow to my art. It's possible instead that my mother would just laugh it off and tell me I have a vivid imagination. But this is a risk I'm unwilling to take, not when it could end with being forced to give up my papercuts, the one thing in my life that I treasure the most.

There's a doorbell, but I decide to knock on the wooden front door in case the Rabbi is asleep. The door opens and a woman stands before me, older than my mother but not elderly. She looks at me expectantly.

Suddenly the words are stuck in my throat. I'm nervous at the thought that I am only steps away from being in Rabbi Kuriel's presence. I take a deep breath and force myself to speak. "Hello. I'm Judith Braverman. I apologize for not calling ahead, but I was hoping to spend a few minutes speaking with Rabbi Kuriel."

The woman is tall with broad shoulders and long medium brown hair streaked with gray. It flows past her shoulders in waves. Her soul shimmers in gold tones, something I've never seen before. It's not blinding like Jeffrey's but it's different than the silver and blue that I usually see. I wonder if the rabbi's soul will look the same.

She steps back and motions for me to come in. Much like the outside, the inside of the house is also modest, and I'm happy to feel cool air surround me. There's a small entryway with a polished wooden staircase straight ahead. I am led into the living room, sparse but comfortable. Two royal blue thick cushioned sofas are at the center, facing one another. A plain glass coffee table is in between the couches and two lighter blue armchairs are on either side. A tall light wood bookcase is against the wall behind one of the sofas, filled with books of all sizes and small objects, pictures, photos in frames, and a silver Chanukah menorah with eight spaces for candles, plus one for the middle.

The woman turns to me. "Why would you like to see my father, Judith?" Her tone is soft and friendly. I might be imagining it, but she appears to be holding back a smile.

I reach in my bag for the folder and hold it out to her. "I've made him a papercut with the *Mi Shaberach*, hoping it will aid in his healing."

She takes it and studies it for a few minutes, her face impassive. I'm hoping she approves of the portion of the prayer I included.

May the One who blessed our fathers
Abraham, Isaac and Jacob
Bless and heal Rabbi Kuriel
Send him a complete healing from the heavenly realms,
A healing of body and a healing of soul,
Speedily, without delay;
and let us say: Amen!

She's taking far longer to read it than my mother. Maybe she's an artist who's examining my technique? Will she find it wanting?

Finally, she closes the folder and motions for me to sit on one of the couches. "It appears that you have many gifts, Judith." She points to the papercut. "This being just one. Am I correct?"

How could she know? I sit there in shock, my mouth open.

She smiles, this time not holding back. "I felt the shimmer when you saw my soul."

"You did? But...but...no one ever has, not even..." I stop before I say Jeffrey's name.

The smile leaves and now her eyes are downcast with sadness. "I wish you could meet with my father because I'm confident he would feel it as well. We are a lot alike."

I wonder if the rabbi has already passed. "Is he gone?"

"No, but soon. He's sleeping right now and he's not in any condition to receive guests. He's in and out of consciousness."

I look down at my lap worried that I'd missed the only chance I'd have to find out more about my gift. Dvorah must notice how disappointed I look. She gently places her hand under my chin and lifts my head so that I am looking into soft green eyes.

"Perhaps I can be of some help to you. What are you hoping to learn from my father?"

My mother attends a Torah study group for Jewish women that Dvorah runs. She describes the rabbi's daughter as "a very learned woman." And Dvorah herself has just told me that she is a lot like her father. I decide it's worth a try.

"This gift of seeing *neshamah*. Why me? And what should I be doing with this?"

She breathes in and I feel the breeze of her exhale. "It is only for The One Who Dwells On High to know why you have been selected to see souls. As for—"

"But not everyone's. Just some people." I'm worried that I've cut her off, but I'm intent on giving her as much information as I have so she can help me make sense of it. I bite my lower lip. "Sorry for interrupting."

I realize I don't know what to call her. Miss Kuriel? Mrs? My mother told me that Dvorah had been married many years ago in Israel and her husband had been killed in a bombing.

She raises both hands with her palms out. "That's fine. I come from a family of interrupters."

I smile. "Me too."

"Judith, I suspect you only can only see *neshamah* on some and not others because Hashem knows which ones you need to see."

I nod. I'd wondered that too.

"As to what you should be doing with this knowledge, I can only guess that the answer will be revealed to you one day. You are still very young and it is likely you will have many experiences where this gift will come to be useful."

Her smile is back and it's the closed-mouthed, knowing one. "Is there anything else you wanted to ask?"

I nod emphatically. Okay, here comes the big one.

"There's this boy I know. Jeffrey. He's a friend. When I first saw him, I could see his soul but it looked nothing like anyone else's." I pause for effect and she fills the silence.

"What do the *neshamah* normally look like?"

"The good ones surround the person and shimmer like fireworks fading into the sky; blue or silver in color." I pause again. "Except for yours. It was golden. Do you know why?"

She purses her lips tightly, her gaze above my head. "Our souls are comprised of levels, with each representing a part of our being. What I guess you normally see is the *nefesh* level, which corresponds to the body. I can only guess that the level of my soul that appeared to you is connected to the mind, the *neshamah*, which is the word we normally use for the entire soul but is really only that one level. It appeared to you because of my gift of prophesy that I inherited from my father. We see and understand things that others cannot."

I remember the article from the newspaper. "Like the future, you mean?"

"Sometimes that, but other things as well…" She trails off. "Now what did you want to ask me about that boy?"

"Oh, yes." I wanted to know more about what she and Rabbi Kuriel could see and feel, but she's right, the most important thing I need to know is about Jeffrey.

"His soul came at me like a blast instead of a shimmer. It was so bright and so powerful that I had to jump back from him. And now every time I see him, it's the same thing."

She is slack-jawed, mouth agape, eyes wide open like she's seen something miraculous. "*Baruch Hashem*," she says, her voice filled with amazement.

As I lean forward to ask about her reaction, I hear the soft tinkle of a bell. Dvorah turns to look toward the staircase and then back at me. She stands.

"Stay here, Judith. My father is awake. Let me see what he needs and I will call down to you if I have to stay with him."

I nod and then hear the tinkle of the bell once again.

I hope against hope that she will return and explain her reaction to my description of Jeffrey's soul. When I don't hear her call to me right away, I stand up to take a closer look at the contents of the shelves behind the couch. There are some photos of a younger Dvorah with Rabbi Kuriel and a woman who must have been his wife. There is another photo of Dvorah with a bearded young man wearing a yarmulke, his arm around her. Could that be her long ago husband?

"He's back asleep."

I turn quickly and there's Dvorah. I'm relieved to see her but a bit embarrassed by my snooping. I hurriedly take my seat.

"Family photos are always interesting, aren't they?" She's smiling as she sits down in one of the armchairs. "Now let's get back to your friend's soul, shall we?"

I again lean forward. "Yes, please. Why did you react the way you did?"

"Well, because it is not every day that a genuine *Tzadik Nistar* is revealed."

"A hidden righteous one?" What could she mean?

Again her eyes light up with pure joy. "Judith, in your lifetime you could see thousands and thousands of souls and never once come across one of the *Lamed Vav Tzadikim*. And yet, here you are a young girl, and you could see in someone that higher level of the soul, the *chayah* or divine life-force. You have indeed found one of the righteous thirty-six!"

I want to address her with some kind of title, but again I'm unsure what to call her. I should have asked my mother how they refer to Dvorah Kuriel in the women's study group. I'll have to remember for later.

I shake my head. I know that there are thirty-six righteous individuals alive at all times who justify the purpose of humankind in the eyes of God, but beyond that... "I'm not sure I understand."

She looks up at the ceiling in thought, her mouth slightly open. "Judith, do you know the story of Oskar Schindler?" she says at last.

"From the Shoah, you mean? He saved Jews, right?"

"Yes, but do you know the story of his life?"

This turn in our conversation confuses me. She's going in so many different directions when all I want to know about is Jeffrey's soul.

She leans back and holds up her index finger, silently asking me to listen and be patient.

"Oskar Schindler was a German Christian and someone who had always looked out for himself. He was a womanizer and a war profiteer. So here's this man, a no-goodnick if there ever was one, and what does he do? He saves the lives of twelve hundred Jews working in his factory, even traveling to Auschwitz to rescue some after they'd been loaded onto the trains."

I nod and smile even though I have no idea why she is telling me this.

"Judith, do you know what happened to Schindler after the war?"

I shake my head.

She surprises me by letting out a little chuckle. "He ended up a *schlemiel*, unlucky and unsuccessful. Nothing he touched after the war came to any good. He and his wife were destitute, and it was only because the Jews he'd saved sent him money that he was able to have anything."

She pauses and I'm still confused.

"Judith, I tell you this because it is very likely that if, God forbid, you'd been alive during that time, that you would have seen that same blast of a *neshamah* coming from Oskar Schindler that you see from the boy you know."

She looks at me expectantly, head tilted, eyes wide. I sit there silently assembling the pieces. "You mean...Oskar Schindler was a *Tzadik Nistar*, one of the thirty-six righteous ones?"

She shrugs. "Possibly."

But then... My mouth flies open when I realize the full meaning of what she is telling me. "Jeffrey? The boy I know? He's one of them?"

She nods. "I cannot say definitely about Schindler, though he fits the profile of someone who lived an unremarkable life before and after fulfilling his fate as a savior. But, the *neshamah* of your friend Jeffrey—it appears just as the ancient mystics said it would."

"But Jeffrey isn't horrible like Oskar Schindler was."

Again I see her knowing smile. "What did Jeffrey say when you told him about his soul?"

"He laughed and teased me. He doesn't believe that I see anyone's *neshamah*. He calls me Super Jew, the crazy artist."

She grins at that. "Ahh, it is just as I thought. The last person who will believe he or she is a *Tzadik Nistar* is the person him or herself. In fact, if anyone goes so far to admit to being one, you know right away they are an imposter."

Again, I hear the tinkling of the bell. The rabbi must be awake. The sound of Dvorah's sigh reaches me as I watch her stand.

"Judith, I must go and stay up there. His time with us is quite short."

"Of course." I rise to leave, wondering if Dvorah's gift will enable her to predict the exact moment when her father will leave this world.

"After *sheloshim*, please come see me again and we'll continue this conversation. We have much to teach one another."

I see myself out as she climbs the stairs, my mind filled with thoughts of Jeffrey and what could be in store for him and for all of us. I'd never wish death on anyone, but seeing how Rabbi Kuriel is so close anyway, I pray that Dvorah's *sheloshim*—her thirty days of mourning—will pass quickly.

CHAPTER SEVEN

Jeffrey

Dear Dani,

The weirdest and most amazing thing happened. I met your brother! He was invited to speak to my Jewish History class, and because he spells his last name like you do (he wrote it on the blackboard), I took a chance and asked him. I didn't know how he'd respond, but he seemed happy that I (kind of) know you.

So I haven't told you this yet, and it's all connected to the thing with your brother, but my father owns a store where people come to get stuff fixed. You know, like screens, radios, devices, computers. It's kind of a crazy place with a small front room that has a counter and a few chairs for people who insist on waiting. The backroom is the actual workshop, with every kind of tool you could imagine, and my personal favorite, a 3-D printer. It prints out any parts we need.

The room is usually a mess with disemboweled electronics everywhere, but it's one of the few places where I feel at peace. I work there three days a week after school and on Sundays. It's not what I want to do for the rest of my life (I have no idea what that is, but it's not that). But for now, it's not a bad job. And it's been useful for me on the Tech Team when something breaks down; I can just fix it.

Anyway, your brother came into my father's store with a device that had a busted screen. (Easy to fix, by the way.) And after I introduced him to my father, your brother invited my whole family for Shabbes dinner this week. He said he regularly has people over and he'd be honored (honored!) to have us.

I stood there behind your brother nodding at my father, praying that he'd say yes. And he did.

Then I did something completely crazy. Crazy because it's something that if I'd thought about it ahead of time, I'd never do. I asked your brother if I could bring a friend.

My father looked at me a bit funny, scrunching up his nose and said to my total embarrassment, right in front of your brother, "A friend? You have a friend?"

Your brother rescued me by quickly answering, "Absolutely you can bring your friend. Who is he?"

Then I had to explain about Judith. Okay, so I guess I have to explain about her to you, too. First of all, she is not, and I repeat not, my girlfriend. So get that notion out of your head. Believe me, it hasn't been easy to convince my parents. They're probably somewhere picking out whatever the groom's family picks out for a wedding that will never happen.

Anyway, I met Judith at this horrible event called a mixer that they make us go to where the boys from my school meet the girls from Judith's school. It's all about wanting us to marry each other. Knowing what was in store for me, I brought a book and sat in a corner reading. Then this girl with curly dark hair kept trying to talk to me, no matter how many times I told her to go away. She told me, get this, that she has seen my soul and it was not like anyone else's. Well I could have told her that, if I believed in something so ridiculous. Anyway, when she made it clear that this was not some nutty (though creative, I have to admit) attempt to find her future husband, we became friends.

Her full name is Judith Braverman, but I call her SJ, Super Jew, because of her soul-seeing thing and also because she makes these Jewish papercuts. I don't know if you've ever seen this stuff. It's like a picture—usually with Hebrew letters and symbols—made from cutting out paper in incredible detail. She's shown me some of them, and she's actually quite good.

So now I know two girls and both are artists. You and SJ. Do you think of yourself as an artist? The visuals you talk about are an art, right?

Getting back to the main story, when I told your brother about Judith (not the soul thing, just that we'd become friends) he said he'd invite her entire family too. You see, Judith's father is the publisher of our community newspaper so he's a big macher, you know, an important person, around here.

I thought my father was going to have a stroke. He just stood there with his mouth open and later asked me how we would get through Shabbes dinner with a college professor and the head of the newspaper. What would we talk about? The food, I answered. Jewish stuff? He was not amused.

So I'll have to write you a full report about this dinner, including whether my father found something to say. Ha, ha.

But before I end this letter that is getting to be as long as the Talmud, I wanted to ask you about your school. It sounds like you hardly go at all. How does that work? What's a project team? I asked Judith and she didn't know. What are your computers like? And, please, please, please, tell me more about the iBrain.

That's it for now (you're probably relieved to read).

Jeffrey

* * *

Professor Fine's house is cluttered with piles of books in the corners of the living room and dining room, and kids' toys everywhere. His wife, Miriam, apologizes every few minutes about "the mess" as she calls it. Almost the entire time we are there, when she's not in the kitchen she is bending down and filling her arms with blocks, dolls, and stuffed animals, and depositing them somewhere down a back hallway. When my mother gets up to help, Miriam's cheeks are pink with embarrassment.

"You're a guest in our home, Mrs. Schwartz," she says. "Please relax. My sister will help."

As if on cue, Rivka, Miriam's sister, collects her own armful of toys. Now there is room to walk without the risk of tripping and falling.

I'm relieved that Miriam is keeping Rivka busy because I figure the less that Rivka Blau, head of the South Ohio Jewish Federation, knows about me, the better. After all, she can drop me from the pen pal program like a hot potato.

The three Fine children, two boys and a girl, are busy running from room to room chasing one another. Judith motions to me to get up from the comfortable leather armchair I'd claimed. Reluctantly, I stand and give her the side eye for pulling me away from my refuge. We are headed toward the children. For some reason Judith thinks this is a good idea.

My father is sitting on a wooden chair, hands folded in his lap, his back straight. I am practically in pain just from the sight of his rigid, uncomfortable position. He is listening to Professor Fine talk about his lecture to my class, filling Mr. Braverman in on the story of how they all came to be invited to this Shabbes dinner.

My mother is standing, looking a bit uncertain about what to do. She turns and walks in the direction of the kitchen.

I sigh to myself as I watch them, grateful that I asked to invite Judith who has once again coaxed me out of my self-imposed isolation and led me to build a Lego castle with the Fine children.

"Were you surprised that Rivka came without her family?" Judith asks me.

"Uh, I guess I didn't notice, but now that you mention it…"

Her voice is almost a whisper and I have to lean over to hear her: "I overhead your mother ask her about it when we were in the kitchen. She said her husband has business in Louisville on Sunday so Rivka suggested he take the children to his sister, who lives there, for the weekend since Rivka has to work on Sunday too."

I nod. "Well, it's probably for the best since my father would be petrified if he had to share Shabbes with the all-powerful

Bernard Blau. It was hard enough to get him to agree to break bread with Professor Fine and your dad, I can't imagine he would have come if he knew the biggest real estate developer in the neighborhood was going to be there."

Shabbes dinner is a grand affair. With the help of Judith and the other women, we are served at least five courses—gefilte fish, chopped liver, chicken soup with carrots and matzo balls, salad, roast chicken with potatoes, and a honey cake dessert. Between each course, Professor Fine talks to us about the week's Torah portion, asking all of us—even the women—to share their thoughts. He also tells us stories about the Baal Shem Tov, the founder of Hasidism. Most of these stories are about a poor, uneducated man—a shepherd or a peddler—who can only praise Hashem in the simplest way, and it always turns out that these simple prayers are the ones the Holy One values most.

My parents have been noticeably quiet. Neither has offered any commentary. But after one of his many stories, this one about a beggar who stopped on his journey to fix the broken wagon of a poor farmer, Professor Fine turns to my father.

"Mr. Schwartz, when you are fixing a man's watch—something that will help him know when it is time to head to the synagogue or leave his place of business to return to his family—isn't it possible that you are perhaps, maybe even a little bit, performing *tikkun olam*, repair of the world?"

My father, seated in yet another wooden chair, his posture still rigid, twists his body and looks down. "Professor Fine," he says in almost a whisper, "the simple act of changing a spring or a wheel can hardly be seen as an act of *tikkun olam*."

Professor Fine's smile is large and genuine. He leans toward my father and emphasizes his point by holding up a finger. "Ah, but, Mr. Schwartz, think about it this way. A young man brings you an old pocket watch that he needs repaired. It belonged to his great-grandfather who lived in a *shtetl* in Poland. The man gives the watch to his son as the son is leaving to move to America. A few years later, comes the Shoah and the entire family remaining in the *shtetl* is murdered."

He pauses, and the mood around the table is changed. Their somber expressions make me wonder if everyone is thinking about some ancestor they lost in the Shoah.

Professor Fine raises his hand, one finger again pointing up. "So," he continues, "isn't it the case that by repairing this heirloom, you, Mr. Schwartz, have reconnected this young man with his past, and with a generation that was effectively wiped off the earth?"

My father sits up taller, his head is tilted in thought. "I-I guess so," he says, his voice still soft.

Professor Fine is now on his feet, gesturing with widespread arms to all of us. "Well then, I can think of no greater act of *tikkun olam* than preserving that which the antisemites wanted to see erased." He turns to Judith's father. "Wouldn't you agree, Mr. Braverman?"

"I would say so, Professor. Very well put."

My mother's smile is matched only by Judith's. What I feel is just a deep sense of relief.

It is getting late, almost ten, but Professor Fine convinces the men, including me, to continue to talk in his study while the women deal with the sleepy children and finish cleaning up.

His study is like something out of a movie. There's a desk piled high with books and papers that cover the entire surface, with a brown leather sofa and a brown armchair that have seen better days. I take the armchair. Professor Fine wheels his desk chair next to the sofa where my father and Mr. Braverman are sitting.

I have no idea what grown men talk about after the Sabbath meal, especially this late at night. In my house, we just usually retreat to our rooms and go to sleep. As I sit there wondering if we're going to be hearing more about the *Bal Shem Tov*, it's Judith's father, and not Professor Fine, who speaks first.

"I assume you've all heard about the President's daughter?"

Our three heads shake at once. While we don't know what he's heard, we do know he's not talking about a daughter of the current president of the GFS. When Jews mention "the

President's daughter," they refer to only one person, the Jewish daughter of a former president of the USA, Marianna Friedrich. As a convert to Judaism, she was the closest thing we've ever had to a Jewish president.

Mr. Braverman's tone is serious and sad. He speaks as he looks down at the floor. "It came over the wire service right before Shabbes. A plane crash into the Florida waters. No one survived."

None of us speak for almost a minute, and then, to my complete surprise, it's my father's voice I hear next.

"May her memory be for a blessing."

Murmurs of amen—or "ahmein" as we say in Hebrew—fill the room.

"She was only, what, seventy years old?" says Professor Fine.

"Seventy-one," Mr. Braverman responds. "Too young."

Professor Fine runs a hand through his curly black hair, smoothing it down. "The timing couldn't be worse, what with everything going on."

Mr. Braverman looks up. "What everything?"

"You know, the beatings, the vandalism."

Judith's father waves a hand in dismissal. "Minor incidents."

"But she was our protection." I'm again shocked that my father has found his voice.

Braverman is shaking his head. "No. Don't listen to those rumors, those *bubbe-meises*, Schwartz."

"I'm not sure he's wrong, Mr. Braverman." Professor Fine has his head in his hands, rubbing his temples. "She stayed close to every administration since the start of the GFS. She made sure we weren't harmed by the school prayer thing. She kept the Christian nation business out of the constitution."

"Yes, yes," Braverman answers with a dismissive wave. "Of course she was an advocate, but remember, we were promised religious freedom, which is why Rabbi Kuriel—may his memory be for a blessing—urged us all to stay here or emigrate from the UPR to the GFS. The government isn't going to turn its back on us just because the President's daughter is gone."

By the looks on their faces, I know my father and Professor Fine don't share Judith's father's faith in government protection. As for me, I've seen too many kids with black eyes and arms in a sling, not to mention all those scary messages on walls and sidewalks, to believe him either.

CHAPTER EIGHT

Dani

I sit on my favorite bench in the park across from the new science and technology museum near the university. The bench is tucked in a corner away from the outdoor playground filled with screaming little kids. I come here every week after my Holograms and Visual Sequencing instruction, just to think and eat my lunch in peace. The diner bot that Kat summons never has any problem locating me.

We have a project due in two weeks and I should be thinking about a topic, but there's something else I'd rather do right now.

"Kat, start an email to Jeffrey Schwartz."

Hey Jeffrey,

Have you ever been to Disneyland? I once got to go when my mother had a work trip to California. Maybe you've been to the one in the GFS, you know, the one that used to be in Florida before…

I pause Kat when I realize I've wandered into controversial territory. This is all so stupid. Everyone knows Disneyworld in Florida had to move to Georgia due to climate change. But I can't say that to Jeffrey or we'll both be thrown out of the program. I have Kat resume the letter.

...before they moved it. Anyway, they have this really old ride there that was even around when my parents were kids, and this song that goes, "It's a small world after all..." Have you ever heard of it? That song came to mind when I read in your email that you'd met my brother. You know, small world, and all that. Now I hope I didn't give you an earworm with that awful song the way I've given myself one.

I'm so eager to hear how your Shabbat dinner went. Oh, and I'm curious. What has my brother told you about me?

What I'm wondering is if he told Jeffrey that I like girls, though I know Binyamin is usually pretty careful about stuff like that. My mom once said my brother tries never to rock the boat, so the GFS won't drum up some reason to stop him from traveling to see us.

I tell Kat to continue, and I phrase the next part of the email carefully.

It's been kind of a crazy few weeks, which is why I didn't write back sooner. I broke up with the person I was dating. It was kind of a mutual thing because we had a major disagreement about an important aspect of our relationship. Basically, I wanted something more and they wanted to keep things more casual.

I was down in the dumps for a while but my friends Ibi, Trey, and Julia, who are on my project team, convinced me it was all for the best and I deserve to get what I really want, and so does this other person. I've decided that the two of us, you know, me and this now ex, should try to be friends, and so far that is working out okay. Maybe because the pressure of this big issue we had was removed, we've been able to get along much better than before. We'll see.

Anyway, I know you said your friend Judith isn't a girlfriend, but in any case she sounds interesting. I looked up papercuts and wow, they are really detailed. Maybe one day I can see a papercut of hers. If Judith isn't your girlfriend, then are you dating anyone else? What are your other friends like?

So now I should get to some of your questions. The way schools work here is all about projects you have to do with your team. Our achievements are based on these projects, including how well we work together. It's supposed to prepare us for what it's going to be like when we get jobs, except in my case, I'm not so sure since I'm probably going to work alone creating all kinds of visis for news sites, or at least I hope I will.

But, for now, my team is pretty amazing. One of our projects is the school's news site where I'm the visual editor. We get together a few times a week for school stuff, but we also just hang out, sometimes with other kids too. I don't know if this is the same for you since you mentioned meeting my brother in your Jewish History class. Here, there's not really school the way there was for my parents, you know, like classes Monday through Friday. I think I'd die of boredom if I had to do that. Instead of teachers, we have "advisors," though some of them are as annoying as what my father tells me teachers were like.

I don't know if I'm describing something you already know about, and if I am, I'm sorry. But you did ask.

My big news about my brother is that he's coming for a visit soon. He comes alone, which is upsetting because we haven't ever met his family, including my niece and nephews, but he can only get one permission visa every six months. He drives his private vehicle to the border where he meets my dad and then they take an AV transport to our house. Private cars are not really popular here.

I stop writing and sigh aloud. This is another place where the insane rules get in the way. What I want to tell Jeffrey is my brother can only visit us by himself, and only twice a year, because of my parents' jobs. My father works for the UPR Border Agency in charge of the entire North Ohio border between the UPR and the GFS and, while my mother doesn't work for the government, she is one of the UPR's best known climate change mitigation specialists working out of an institute at Ohio State. Basically, the GFS regards my parents as threats to their precious country. This is why I've never met my niece and nephews and why my parents have been kept from their own grandchildren. The only reason Binyamin can visit at all is because his sister-in-law, the same one who got me into the pen pal program, is high up at the Jewish agency in South Ohio. But I can't say any of this to Jeffrey.

Instead I sign off the email and send it, then I have Kat order me an AV so I can get home. There's one circling the park, so I don't have to wait long.

CHAPTER NINE

Judith

The kiddish lunch after Saturday morning Shabbes services is a big deal with tons of food and people milling around catching up on the week's news about their families, jobs, and school. I hear a few discussing the Torah portion and the rabbi's sermon or *drash* but they are exceptions. Mostly the women are talking about which baby kept them up at night, which son came home with a perfect test score, and who might be a good match for their daughters (though luckily my mother is not part of those conversations). The men talk about work even though they're really not supposed to today, and about politics. There's a new Jewish candidate running for city council from our district, a young man, Solomon Herschel, but he doesn't seem to be very popular among this crowd.

"He's riling everyone up with his talk of violence," I overhear someone say.

"How long can we look the other way? It's only the goyim who say 'turn the other cheek.' For us, it's an eye for an eye. Maybe it's time we start following that?"

"Ach, a few ruffians here and there. It's not like we haven't lived through that kind of thing for centuries."

It's all I can do to keep my mouth shut before I blurt out something like, "It's not just a few. You should see Hannah's photos." But I know I'd be shushed and sent on my way. Because, after all, what does a teenage girl know?

Once I've passed through the food line and filled my plate, I look around and see Hannah sitting in a corner at a small round table. She waves me over, her arm jerking toward the table in an insistent movement. I nod and make my way through the knots of people who stand together balancing plates in one hand while gesturing in conversation with the other.

"Finally," she says when I sit down.

"You know how it gets here." I twist my body around to see if I can catch Jeffrey's eye. I wave and he smiles and raises the hand that isn't holding a plate.

"You know, Judith," Hannah says, "you're not convincing me that he's just a friend when the first thing you do once you sit down is call him over."

I shrug and shake my head at her. "Then you'll just have to believe what I've told you a hundred times. He's just a friend."

"Hey," says Jeffrey as he deposits his plate on the table. It's piled even higher than mine. "Jews and food, gotta love it."

"Good Shabbes, Hannah." Isaac Leventhal's deep voice reaches us as he comes up from behind Jeffrey.

Hannah is grinning from ear to ear, which makes me smile. Isaac slides a chair over from the next table and now there are four of us. I make a point of complimenting Isaac on his father's *drash*, knowing that it's the polite thing to do.

"SJ," says Jeffrey, as he holds a piece of whitefish on a fork and points it at me, "you *would* be the one of us who actually listened."

Instead of taking offense, Isaac laughs. "What does SJ stand for, Schwartz?"

I blush when Jeffrey says Super Jew. Hannah bursts out laughing and Isaac chuckles.

"Well, that explains why you actually listen to my father's *drashot* instead of nodding off like everybody else."

I'm starting to see why both Hannah and Jeffrey like this boy. He's sweet and easygoing, plus he has a sense of humor. I guess my reading of his soul was accurate. Plus, I know Hannah finds him very attractive, and I can see why. He's tall, has thick, wavy light brown hair and soft brown eyes. He and Hannah make a striking couple.

There are not many opportunities for the four of us to talk like this, especially out of earshot of our parents. I don't want my chance to slip away by spending our time talking about school and a lot of other silly topics. So I just launch right in.

"Isaac, do you agree that the death of the President's daughter is a bad sign for us?"

His answer to this question will tell me a lot about him. The three of us face him and wait. I realize that both Hannah and Jeffrey are wondering the same thing as me.

Isaac appears to be looking past the three of us as he quietly responds, "Yes."

I can feel the tension in my body relax and there's an exhale of relief from both Hannah and Jeffrey.

"Well now there are four of us," says Jeffrey. "Well, five if you count Professor Fine."

"The one who came to our class?" Isaac asks.

"Yes, it's a long story but I ended up at his home for Shabbes dinner last week and that's when we found out she'd died in the plane crash."

"All the beatings and the broken windows and stuff," says Isaac, still somewhat looking past us. "It's getting worse, and I'm worried that this is just the beginning. Without the President's daughter, we have no one looking out for us."

I see Hannah begin to reach for Isaac's hand, which is lying open on the table, and then she remembers herself and jerks her hand back. Even that simple act of comfort is not allowed, and if anyone saw it we'd be separated immediately.

"I have pictures," says Hannah. She looks at me and Jeffrey first and then turns all her attention to Isaac. "I catch whatever I can before it's cleaned up. I even have some videos."

"Wow!" says Jeffrey and blows out a soft whistle. "Too bad your father wouldn't publish them, SJ."

I roll my eyes. "He'd call them a waste of space."

"Where do you keep them?" asked Isaac.

"They're safe. Offloaded from my device onto memory dots and hidden away." She sighs. "But I'm not sure there's anything I can do with them."

"What about Professor Fine?" I ask Jeffrey. "Could he do something with them?" I lean forward and whisper, "Maybe take them to the UPR when he visits?"

Isaac's eyes are wide. "He goes to the UPR?"

Jeffrey nods. "Twice a year to see his parents and his sister. She's my pen pal."

Isaac squints in confusion. I decide there's too little time left before one of our parents comes over to put an end to this little gathering. Jeffrey can explain all that later. "Would he be able to bring the dots over the border?"

"No," says Isaac, "he'll be scanned and they'll turn up and take a look at what's on them. Same thing if they're printed out."

"At least he can tell people what's happening, right?"

"We can't put this all on him," says Jeffrey. "Dani kind of implied in her email they never know if he'll be granted the visa each time he applies to go north."

"Hold on," says Hannah, excitement in her voice. She's practically bouncing in her chair. "How suspicious would it be if Professor Fine brought one of Judith's papercuts to show his family? You know, just a piece of art?"

I tilt my head at Hannah, wondering what she's getting at. She gives me a meaningful look, nodding furiously at me. I open my mouth and breathe out an "Ohhh" because the meaning behind her question is suddenly clear to me.

"What's going on here?" asks Jeffrey, his head moving back and forth between me and Hannah.

Isaac raises his arms in confusion. "Huh? A papercut?"

"Uh-oh," says Jeffrey. "Party time's over. *Rebbetzin* at two o'clock."

Isaac's mother, the rabbi's wife, is walking toward us. Hannah and Isaac turn toward her. I see Hannah's body stiffen.

My words tumble out quickly before Isaac's mother gets any closer. "Let me and Hannah work this out and we'll fill you in after. We'll make sure that any help Professor Fine gives us doesn't get him in trouble."

CHAPTER TEN

Dani

It always amazes me that Binyamin owns a private car, something only he and Miriam drive. It's not even a shared. No one here would think of having their own car. First, of course, there's the cost of fuel. Doesn't matter if it's gas or electric. Then there's the stigma of being looked down on for contributing to the worsening climate.

But that's the difference between our country and Binyamin's. I can't even use the term "climate change" in my emails to Jeffrey, which of course speaks volumes about the driving habits of people in the GFS, among other things.

My dad and I are sitting in his Border Security Department's AV on our way south to meet my brother. It's a small six-passenger transport, not a larger one with white boards all around and a conference table for meetings like the vans that my father and his coworkers usually get. Binyamin will park in a lot at the checkpoint and after he's scanned and practically dissected by the GFS goons, he'll be waved through by my dad's guards.

My heart races with excitement at the thought of seeing him, my only sibling. My mom isn't crazy about the ever-present yarmulke on his head or the white *tzitzit* fringes that peek out below the bottom of his shirt. She wishes he'd give up the whole "Orthodox thing" as she calls it and just go back to being her son, Ben. Then he and Miriam and the kids could live with us here in Columbus (or whatever it'll soon be called), and we wouldn't have to worry that they won't give him his visa the next time he wants to visit. Then, and only then, can we be a real family.

I sit quietly in the transport watching a visicast on holograms and then ask Kat to switch to the meditation audio that Binyamin recorded for me. Because every school here requires that we learn mindful breathing and meditative focus from the age of five, I've been doing this forever. It's become a part of me, like brushing my teeth or washing my hair. But Binyamin added a whole Jewish twist to it with his meditations on the five levels of the soul or *neshamah*, as he calls it. When he first talked about it, it sounded silly, but because he's my brother and I hardly get to see him, I said I'd try it out as a way to begin to understand why he cares so much about this stuff.

Now I love it. Not only does it help me feel close to my brother, it also gets me to meditate on the different aspects of myself—my body, my mind, my emotions, the whole of the life-force going through me. Binyamin made it a little more palatable for me by talking about The Creator instead of God, which is helpful because I can deal with a creator but not the idea of a dude up above treating us all like a bunch of puppets.

I laughed out loud when I listened to Kat read me Jeffrey's latest email about his friend Judith who claims to see people's souls. I wonder if Binyamin thinks that all his meditating has enabled him to do that.

As I lean back on the comfortable seat of the AV, my relaxed focus on the soul's level of emotion in the mediation fills my mind and helps me stop worrying about the whole tense standoff between my mom and my brother that's likely to flare up again during this visit. Even after all these years she won't give an inch and he's gotten very good at tuning her out. My dad leaves the room when she starts in, or, when he can't, he changes the subject. I stay quiet and try to silently communicate my support to Binyamin. It's not that I can't see my mom's point about the family being separated, it's just that if I don't respect the choices my brother has made, then how can I expect him or my parents to respect mine?

When we finally arrive at the border, Binyamin's hug is warm and comforting, like the embrace of a soft winter coat on a cold day. We let it last a little longer than a regular hug and then we spend a few seconds grinning at one another.

On the trip home, we share the AV with some guards coming off their shift. My dad checks his app and is relieved to see that we're the first stop.

I lean against my brother and he puts his arm around me. My dad has a hand on Binyamin's shoulder. The three of us sit like this for most of the trip, trading little bits of news about school and work.

"Lemme save all the stuff about Miriam and the kids for home, so I won't have to repeat it to Mom."

"Probably better than listening to her lecture you again," I say.

"She lectures me?" Binyamin asks in mock surprise. "I hadn't noticed."

I hear my dad chuckle and I pull closer to my brother, laughing into his coat.

* * *

I can tell my mom's trying to be on her best behavior. She sits patiently at the table while Binyamin chants the blessing before we eat and then later the blessing once the meal is finished. I can see her practically squirming in her chair waiting for the prayer to end. I have to admit the last one he chants goes on a very long time.

"I imagine you've heard about the President's daughter?" my brother asks, his head turned toward my dad.

"The President's daughter," my mother repeats and ends with a sigh, her head shaking. "You mean, the Jewish sellout of the worst president the USA ever had? Yes, we heard. I hope she rots in hell."

Now it's Binyamin's turn to sigh. "Mom, she protected us in the GFS. I know not everyone sees it that way, including many of the people in my community, but a few of us are very concerned."

I imagine that Binyamin is probably referring to the important men he knows, and certainly not the women. But maybe I'm wrong. Binyamin talks about the women in his family, especially Miriam and her sister, with great respect. I decide to ask him, but I'm shut out by my mother's usual lecture.

"So you continue to stay there with your wife and my grandchildren, knowing that your great protector can no longer help you? How is that not *meshuganah*, as you would say? What kind of father and husband does that, Ben?"

My father is quiet as he collects the dinner plates. Mom knows all his diversions once these arguments begin.

"Steven, sit down." She motions to my dad's chair. "Fine House, clean up dinner."

The bot rolls out of the kitchen and begins to collect our plates, glasses, and utensils. My father is back in his chair with his elbows on the table, his head in his hands.

I decide to jump into the fray. "Mom, Binyamin's only here a short time. Do we have to spend it having the same old argument?"

My mother leans in my direction. "Dani, you lead a sheltered life here. You get to be who you want to be and learn what you want to learn. There's no one waiting on the corner to hit you over the head or call you a dirty Jew, thank God. Wouldn't you want the same for your nephews and niece?"

I'm struck by the fact that my mother mentioned God since she's an atheist. "Thank God?" is all I can say.

"Figure of speech."

Binyamin rolls his eyes and mutters something in Hebrew I don't understand. I think about Binyamin's three little kids growing up in the GFS, following a religion that treats girls differently than boys and probably doesn't accept anyone queer. That's my problem with this argument my family has each time my brother visits. I can see both sides and I have no idea what to do about it.

I leave the table and head to my room.

"Dani, wait up," my brother says. I turn and see him walking toward me. "I want to spend a little time with you, if that's all right."

I smile at him and nod. I can't remember the last time my brother was in my room. It usually isn't one of the places he goes when he visits. I've wondered if it was some kind of religious modesty thing about not seeing women's private places, but tonight here he is sitting in my desk chair while I face him perched on the side of my bed.

Does he think my sky-blue room, messy with screens of all sizes and dirty laundry, is childish? There are jpgs on the walls. Pictures of my friends; famous queer folk in history like Sylvia Rivera, Audre Lorde, and Harvey Milk; and some of my own work. Binyamin looks around at the scene and smiles at a picture of rain falling into a pond.

"This is one of yours, isn't it?"

"Yes, last year after the long heat wave. I titled it *Relief.*"

"You think it was hot here, try going a bit south," he says. "The visual is beautiful, Dani. You're very talented."

I look down at the floor and murmur my thanks, then face him. My words come out in a torrent. "Does Jeffrey agree with you? You know, about the President's daughter?"

My brother's eyes crinkle with happiness at the mention of my pen pal's name. "He's a good boy, your Jeffrey. He was in the room with the men after Shabbes dinner when we heard the news. By the look on his face I'd say he agrees with me, as does his father."

"Is it really not safe for you, for Jews, there?"

Binyamin puts his hands together, palm to palm, and points the tops of his fingers at me. "I'm not sure yet. We'll have to see."

In the brief silence that follows, I have to literally stop myself from running to him and bolting him to my desk chair, forbidding him to go back there. I'm starting to wonder if there really is something to all the stuff my mother yells at him.

"Dani," he begins. "I brought you something and I want you to listen to me very carefully when I talk to you about it."

"Okay." I have no idea where this is going. He reaches into his suit jacket and pulls out a book, navy blue and quite worn. We don't use many hard copy books anymore, but I know that isn't the case in the GFS. Maybe this is a book he wants me to read. But no. He opens the book and takes out a folded piece of paper that looks a bit like Swiss cheese. It has holes all over. He clears a space on my desk, moving a screen, and lays it flat.

I walk over to see a picture of a simple house with tall trees surrounding it that's cut into the paper with Hebrew letters and some other symbols I don't recognize.

"Dani, these are papercuts. Papercutting is a Jewish artform that's centuries old. Did Jeffrey tell you about his friend Judith?"

Yes, of course, that's what this is. It's a piece of Judith's art. I nod to Binyamin and lean forward to examine the paper over Binyamin's shoulder. Even though I have no idea what any of it means, I can appreciate the artistry. It's gorgeous. The detail is so intricate. How could she possibly do this?

"Does she use a computer?"

"Not at all. Just paper, an Exacto knife, scissors, and maybe a pencil to draw the design."

It's so delicate that I'm afraid if I touch it, it'll fall apart. "Is this mine to keep?"

Binyamin swivels toward me. "Yes, but this is much more than a gift, Dani. It's a way for Jeffrey and Judith to communicate with you so they can say some things that they can't put in an email."

"You mean like a secret code?"

"That's exactly what I mean."

"But I don't read Hebrew. I have no idea what this says. I mean, I guess I can look it up online."

"The literal meaning is not important. But you do need to understand how to decipher the message."

I nod. "Okay, explain it to me."

He points to the paper. "I imagine you don't have a copy of the Weissberg Torah translation in the house?"

I shrug. "Probably not."

"That's okay, why don't you pull it up on the screen." He looks around my room. "Where's your computer?"

I pull my iBrain out of my pocket and attach it to the side of my head. "Right here," I say and point to it.

Binyamin opens his mouth, eyebrows raised, and lets out a breath. "Oh, okay. I'm always amazed at the difference between our two countries when it comes to technology."

"I'm always amazed at the amount of censorship in the GFS. You should see the list of topics I can't mention in my emails to Jeffrey. And anyway, why are you still using email?"

The only reaction from my brother is a sigh followed by the shaking of his head. "Is there a screen?" he asks.

"Kat, get me the uh…" I look over at my brother.

"Weissberg translation of the Torah."

I repeat that to Kat and the image pops up in front of us without the use of a screen. These days it's becoming less and less necessary to use or own screens since AR, augmented reality, enables images to appear on their own without the need for those clunky, old glasses. The iBrain has made them obsolete. As I look at the home page for the Weissberg thing I'm reminded that I need to recycle all the old screens cluttering up my room.

"Great," says Binyamin as his eyes scan the projected image, "now we need to figure out where to look and Judith has embedded that in the papercut." He studies the paper with one finger scanning the letters and picture. "Ah, here it is." He points to three Hebrew letters in the top right corner. I'm still completely in the dark.

"Give me a paper and pen and I'll explain it," he says.

Since the UPR is trying desperately to save the planet we try not to use things like paper that are linked to deforestation, especially given how little forest we have left from all the fires and the logging. But when I do come across something tacked to a wall somewhere, I take it so it can be reused. Since we don't use paper, pens are not easy to find, but I happen to have an old stylus that doubles as a pen. I find what Binyamin needs and then watch as he slowly writes out a row of Hebrew letters across the page from right to left and then a row of numbers, beginning with one, under each letter. After 10, he skips to 20, then 30 and so on until he reaches 100. Then he skips right to 200, and finally finishes at 400. Now I'm starting to get it. The letters in the papercut are codes for the numbers. But then what do the numbers mean?

"Dani, these are the numerical values for each letter in the Hebrew alphabet. Once you get past ten, you need to combine letters to write the numbers in between. So, eleven would be written using this letter," he points to a tiny letter that looks kind of like an apostrophe, "and this one." He points to the first letter, that's a fancy kind of X.

"I get it, but then what? How do I figure out the message?"

"That's the next step. These letters at the top right corner are the clue. You need three numbers to get you to the right section of the Torah; the book number, the chapter, and the verse. So you match these three Hebrew letters to the numbers on this paper." He lifts up the sheet with his writing and hands it to me. "Now tell me, of these three letters in the upper right corner, what numbers do they represent? And remember, Hebrew is read right to left."

I sigh out loud. As if this wasn't hard enough. But I'm determined since I know Jeffrey and Judith wouldn't have gone to all this trouble if these messages weren't important.

I look closely and see the first letter is that fancy X. "Book one?"

Binyamin smiles. "That's right. Genesis. There are five books in the Torah, so the first letter will always be one of these." He tugs the paper back from me and runs a finger over the first five letters. I nod and take the paper back, ready to figure out the chapter. It's something that looks a little like a V. "Chapter nine?"

"Very good. Now tell me the verse."

The letter looks like the number seven with a line at the bottom, or a backward letter c. Actually, it doesn't look like anything I've ever seen before. How Judith is able to make these tiny cuts with just a scissor is nothing short of a miracle. I look back at Binyamin's chart. "Verse two, right?"

"Yes, so now ask your computer, or whatever it is, to go there."

I give Kat the command and then the image we see is filled with verses in both Hebrew and English. They appear to have something to do with animals and Noah's ark. I quickly scan the words and frown. "Why does it say man and only talk about sons? Weren't there any daughters or were they just not important enough to list here?"

"Dani, can we not have this conversation right now when I'm trying to get you through these codes?"

I shrug and shake my head. "You know, I don't agree with everything Mom says to you, but you gotta admit when it comes to this stuff, she kind of has a point."

Binyamin actually rolls his eyes at me. "First things first, okay?"

I nod. "All right, what am I looking for here?"

"Now we go back to the papercut and figure out how they embedded the message. This gets a bit tricky, so follow along closely."

He points to the bottom of the papercut where a long line of smaller Hebrew letters are cut into the sheet.

"What does that say?" I ask.

"Nothing. It's just a line of seemingly random letters, but actually it's going to get you the message."

He walks me through this part instead of asking me to figure it out myself. I'm glad he's taking a break from acting like a teacher since this part is really difficult. It turns out that when you assign each of these random Hebrew letters to a number using my brother's chart, it gives you a sequence to follow.

"The first three Hebrew letters on the papercut are four, five and six," says my brother. "You see that on the chart?"

I look and nod.

"Good. That means the message begins with T-H-E, which are the fourth, fifth and sixth letters in the verse."

"Okay, that's pretty easy." I smile at him. Maybe I can do this.

Now he's back to being a teacher and asks me to tell him the number of the next Hebrew letter, which I do.

"Yes, that's ten," he says. "And the next number?"

I look closely and squint at the chart. "It's another three. Does that mean I go back to the third letter?"

My brother shakes his head. "No. Take a look here." He points with his pinky to a small space separating the Hebrew three from the number after it. "This space means that you add the numbers of the last two letters. So that's ten and three, which gets to the thirteenth letter in the verse. Do you see that?"

I let out a breath and slump down in my seat. "I'll never be able to do this on my own after you leave."

Binyamin puts down the papers and lays his hands on my shoulders. "Dani, you must. Just practice and keep at it. I don't have to tell you how important this is."

I walk over to my bedroom window and look at the leaves on the tree in our yard. They sway a bit as I watch them. I take a few breaths, the way we've been taught to do at school during morning and afternoon meditation. In through the nose, out through the mouth.

I wonder if I should tell my friends about the code. I bet they'd be all over it and want to help me. That's when I realize I don't have to do this alone. I can ask Julia to write a program that'll decipher the code so I won't have to tie my brain in knots.

I turn back to my brother who is sitting quietly waiting for me to say something.

"Would it be okay if I told my friends about this? I think one of them can write a sequence that could decipher the code automatically."

Binyamin stands and stretches his arms above his head, moving his shoulders up and down. This whole thing must be making him tense.

"You can tell a few of your friends but please ask them to be discreet. If word got out back home, Judith and Jeffrey would be in more trouble than you can even imagine. And of course you'd both be kicked out of the Pen Pal Program. Plus, I'm not sure I'd be able to get another visa to visit again."

The thought of never seeing him again weighs on me. I feel it in my chest and my stomach. Nausea, heat. I touch my forehead. It's warm.

Binyamin points to my bed. "Sit, Dani. You look like you're going pass out."

We spend a few more minutes in silence and then Binyamin speaks quietly, almost in a whisper. "Let's finish this, okay?"

We work through the remaining Hebrew letters, deciphering the whole message. It's actually rather short. Just one sentence. "T-H-E-Y-W-A-N-T-U-S-O-U-T.

"They want us out?" I ask my brother. "Who wants who out?"

"They want the Jews out."

"Who? Why?"

"For the same reason they've always wanted us out. They're antisemites."

"Wait, I'm confused. Didn't the GFS invite Orthodox Jews to settle there?"

"Originally, yes. But some of us are concerned that it's beginning to change, especially now that Marianna Fredrich, may her memory be for a blessing, is no longer around to stop them."

"To stop the government?"

"Dani, I don't know. It's not yet clear. The only thing I know is that the hateful graffiti and beatings by street thugs have gotten worse. Even at the border this time, as I was being searched, there were comments about my *yarmulke* and *tzitzit*, and let's just say they weren't very flattering."

I look over at the little white strings peeking out from under the bottom of his shirt and resting against his pants pockets. "Did you say something or complain?"

"Not if I wanted to cross over to see you and our parents."

"Fucking bastards."

"Hey, there's no need for that kind of language, even if it is well-deserved. But I'd appreciate it if you could refrain in my presence."

I cover my face with my hands and breathe out audibly. "Sure," I mutter through my fingers.

CHAPTER ELEVEN

Jeffrey

Isaac is filling me in on today's Talmud discussion that I seemed to have missed because I spent the whole period in my head, alternating between the hidden codes in Judith's papercut—I gotta hand it to her and Hannah, they are two smart cookies—and counting the minutes until I could walk home from school with Isaac. It seems he's becoming somewhat of an obsession, which, of course, means that *I* am not a very smart cookie since he is clearly hyper-focused on Hannah. But what's the harm in a little daydreaming? Right? Plus, because of my connection to Judith, and hers to Hannah, Isaac and I are becoming actual friends.

As we walk away from the school building Isaac turns to me, gesturing with both hands. "There are times, Jeffrey, when the Talmud actually surprises me in a good way. Like today, I mean, usually I have to run theological rings around some of this stuff about men and women. I just can't believe that someone as amazing as Hannah could be anything but my equal, maybe even my better."

There it is again. Hannah. But he has a point. Judith Braverman, reader of souls and artist extraordinaire, is clearly a superior being, especially when compared to a *schlemiel* like me.

Isaac continues to expound on the Talmud, and even though I confess that I should have been listening to what I'd missed the first time around, I am instead preoccupied by his light brown eyelashes and how they are a shade paler than his light brown eyes. His face is smooth, and I wonder about the arguments he must be having with his father the rabbi about his decision to shave. Those long sideburns, nicely shaped below his ears, were likely the compromise. Hashem was no doubt having a very good day when He created this perfection.

We reach the corner where he has to turn and I continue straight on toward home. He points in the direction I'd be walking. "You know what, I'll walk a bit with you so I can finish this thought." And on he goes. What a *mensch*.

"That whole discussion about requiring that a woman give verbal consent to sexual relations with her husband. I would have never expected such a modern view."

Yeah, I think, Simeon Rausch must have missed that day. He was probably too busy pushing some guy against a wall and forcing him to put his mouth down there. Ugh, just the thought of what was my horrible first sexual experience makes me close my eyes, a look of disgust unavoidably coming through.

"Jeffrey, you okay? You look sick?"

"Yeah, I guess a little bit. I'm kind of nauseous all of a sudden."

Isaac puts a hand on my shoulder and warmth spreads down my arm. "I can walk you all the way."

"No, that's all right. I'll be fine. I'm close to my dad's shop. I'll go there."

After a few more reassurances, Isaac turns and walks back toward the corner where we normally part ways. I'm relieved to have gotten through my little white lie and annoyed with myself for conjuring up the memory of Simeon pushing down on my shoulders, his voice rough like his hands when they grasp the sides of my head. The sound of his zipper and then the push toward his crotch, and only two words he spits out, "Do it!"

Once he's finished and I stand, wanting to get away from him as fast as possible, I'm again pushed to the wall. "You tell anyone and your life is over! Do you understand?"

I nod and his grip on me eases. I run as fast as I can down the hall toward the first bathroom I can find.

As I sit in the stall, my mind is pulling me in opposing directions. There's the utter disgust at Simeon. His hairy face, arms, and crotch. The acrid smell of onions and piss. His caveman voice and the hideous grunt when he comes. Then there's me. My first time with another boy. The feeling of him in my mouth. The excitement in spite of the circumstance.

I stand and open the toilet, emptying the contents of my stomach. My hatred of Simeon gives way to my disgust with myself. How could I have possibly seen anything positive in this?

Unfortunately, this isn't the only opportunity I'll have to ask myself that question. Simeon continues to corner me every few weeks, ending our encounter with the same stupid threat. I never speak, I just nod that I won't tell. There's not any verbal consent from me to him and there never will be.

This horrible walk down memory lane is suddenly interrupted by the shouts of loud male voices behind me. I can't understand any of the actual words, but when I turn around I see three big guys surrounding someone. Slowly I walk in their direction, hiding behind parked cars and bushes so I won't be seen.

Now the words are clearer. I hear "Dirty Jew boy" and "Tell Daddy it's time to leave." Oh no, it's an attack. I quickly snap a photo making sure to keep myself out of their sight. I take a video so their voices are recorded. And then I see who it is they are beating up, his light brown hair and the navy school jacket and the beautifully shaped sideburn. It's Isaac!

Before I can think about what I'm doing, I'm running toward them, yelling, "Get away. I've called the police. You're all going to jail. Get off him."

It actually works. They stop. Three football player types, broad shoulders, no necks, red "GOD FEARING BOYS" caps on their heads.

They run toward me and I'm wondering if I'm the next one who'll be bleeding on the ground. I can't believe I didn't use my device and really call the police. I hear, "Jew faggot," and before I can ask myself how they could know, my legs are knocked out from under me and my cheek slams against the pavement. I look up to see what's coming next, but all I can see are their backs walking away from me and from poor Isaac who is probably hanging by a thread. That thought is enough to get me up on my feet, even though it's an effort to walk without swaying.

Isaac is lying in a patch of dirt. There's blood trickling from his nose and his forehead. His yarmulke is who knows where. His jacket is twisted around his body, filthy from the mud. His arms and legs are splayed at odd angles.

I lean over him and take his hand so I can hold his wrist. There's a pulse. His lips move. He's trying to talk, which fills me with relief because now I know he's breathing. "Shh," I tell him. "It's over. They're gone." He needs to get to the hospital.

I finally reach for my device to get a picture of his injuries and to hit the police button. Once I know they are on their way, I realize I need to call his parents. But something holds me back. I've never spoken directly to the rabbi. So I do the next best thing. I call Judith.

CHAPTER TWELVE

Judith

"I don't know why Jeffrey called me and not the rabbi," I tell Dvorah as I sit in her kitchen sipping the peppermint tea she has served me. Two pieces of cinnamon *ruchelach* pastries sit on a small plate next to my cup.

Like the rest of the house, the kitchen is neat and uncluttered, very different from the constant mess in my house with dishes piled high in two sinks, jars and bags crowding counters, and cabinets hanging open or slightly ajar. This kitchen is painted a pale yellow with light wood cabinets. The *fleishig* or meat side is clearly distinguishable from the *milchig* or dairy side by two ceramic figures of a chicken and a triangular wedge of yellow Swiss cheese, each on a small shelf set on walls above the counter.

Dvorah leans back in her chair. She is dressed simply in a lilac blouse and a dark gray skirt. A thin silver chain around her neck is hiding under the blouse whatever charm or symbol she keeps close to her heart. I wonder what it is.

"I can understand Jeffrey's hesitation," she says. "Rabbi Leventhal and his wife are imposing figures in our community. Sometimes leaders hold themselves apart to make sure they retain their stature. It's useful when they are asked to render a judgment, whether theological or personal, though the two of course are linked." She smiles.

"Is that how your father, Rabbi Kuriel, may his memory be for a blessing, acted?"

Still smiling, she purses her lips and shakes her head slightly. "No. Papa was always in the mix, playing on the floor with the children, visiting the men at their businesses, and welcoming Shabbes at a table crowded with people. He went about it in a different way. But neither one is right or wrong, Judith. It depends on the leader's temperament and the times they live in."

The image of Isaac Leventhal comes into my mind. Not the bruised and battered Isaac I visited in the hospital with Jeffrey and Hannah, but the open, friendly, handsome Isaac I see at the Shabbat kiddish. He is destined to take his father's place one day and I wonder if he'll be more like Rabbi Leventhal or Rabbi Kuriel. I can't imagine that someone with such a soul would hold himself apart or that Hannah, if they should marry, which I'm increasingly certain they will, would want it that way.

"Isaac told us the police refused to do anything, even after his father went to visit the captain himself."

Dvorah sighs. "Yes, I heard. They think a public prosecution would only serve to inflame the antisemites when in reality not prosecuting will just give them license to continue what they're doing. Sadly, in this way, the police have become their enablers."

I realize in that moment that Dvorah is not speaking as an ordinary member of our community bemoaning the state of affairs in Cincinnati. She has the gift of prophesy, of seeing what lies ahead. I put down my cup, sit up and lean forward.

"Dvorah, can you see how much worse it's going to get for us here in the GFS? Jeffrey says that because the president's daughter, may her memory be for a blessing, is gone, we have lost our protector."

She is quiet for a full minute. Her head is tilted up, her eyes half-closed. I don't know if she is thinking how to answer me or if she is actually seeing something in response to my question. I sit and wait, sipping my tea, the last whiffs of steam tickling my nose and the scent of peppermint keeping me company like a friend. If there's anyone who can be patient because they understand the power of a gift like Dvorah's, it's me.

At last she comes out of what I can only think of as a trance.

"Judith, you know how you describe your gift from Hashem as imperfect because you can only see some souls and not others? Well, in some respects, it is the same for me."

"You can only see the future sometimes and not others?" I pray this is not one of those times.

"No. The imperfection of my gift is that I can only see broad outlines of what is to come, not a lot of the specifics. I cannot tell you what you will have for dinner in a week's time or how many children you will have. In Hashem's infinite wisdom, humans have been granted free will so that I cannot know ahead of time exactly what choices you or anyone will make in their lives."

I know from the reading I do on my own to inform my art that the concept of free will goes back to Genesis and the Garden when Hashem first made man and woman. Their act of eating from the Tree of Life could be seen as the first example of free will.

I want to let Dvorah know that I understand what she means so I share what I would consider my imperfect thoughts on the subject. "I have always believed that Hashem's plan for us includes our need to choose a life that favors good over evil and that the only way we can do so was to have been banished from the Garden."

"Yes, I see it that way as well."

I am proud that she agrees with my interpretation. The feeling of joy and relief is much greater than any test grade I've ever received from a teacher.

"To return to your question, Judith, what my gift does allow me see is that there are hard times ahead for us. If I were one of those women looking into a crystal ball, like you might read about in a book, I would say something like 'dark times in the days to come.'"

She speaks these words in a deep, farcically ominous voice and then breaks into a big smile that quickly fades. "I believe you and your friend Jeffrey will very much be needed to get us through what is to come, though I cannot tell you exactly what that will mean."

Her words hit me like a blow to my stomach. I am no heroine. I am no Queen Esther who has the power and the wisdom to save her people. And Jeffrey, *Tzadik Nistar* though he may be, could not even bring himself to call the Rabbi. How can he be expected to rise to the occasion in times of trouble?

Dvorah reaches over and touches my arm. Her touch is consoling, comforting.

"I see the worry on your face, Judith. But remember what is written in *Pirkei Avot* when Rabbi Tarfon teaches that it is not your responsibility to finish the work, but you are not free to desist from it either. And also remember from your own recounting of recent events to me, when Jeffrey saw Isaac being beaten he did not call for help immediately. Instead he was compelled to run shouting at the antisemites, which caused them to stop their attack on Isaac. Think about that, Judith. It was a rare example of an act of free will by Jeffrey inspired by the hidden responsibility granted to him by the One Whose Infinite Wisdom We Cannot Know."

* * *

Isaac sits at what has now become our weekly Shabbat kiddish table. His right arm is in a sling and there is still a bandage on his forehead. He tells us his stitches will be coming out on Monday and he's hoping the scar they leave will be faint.

Hannah brings him a plate of food. Ever since she learned about the attack she has been alternating between despair, worry, and anger. Today must be a day of worry because the look on her face as she lays the plate down in front of Isaac makes me think she is seconds away from bursting into tears.

Isaac must see it too because he smiles and reaches out his good hand but then retracts it, remembering the prohibition against touch. "Don't be so sad, Hannah. I'm feeling fine. Another five weeks and this cast comes off and I'll be my old annoying self again."

He's interrupted by the arrival of Jeffrey who is struggling with four cups filled with grape juice. I stand and relieve him of two of them.

When I look down at the contents of the two white paper cups in my hands, I notice that one is the color of the red-purple grape juice we always get and the other is a shade more purple. I sniff it.

"Jeffrey, you got wine?"

"Shhh, SJ. Don't make a big *megillah*, okay?" He busies himself pouring a wine-grape juice mixture into two cups and gives one to Isaac. "It helps with the pain," he says looking at me.

Hannah rolls her eyes at him, takes a gulp from her juice and then pours some of Jeffrey's mixture into her cup.

"Thank you for sharing," she tells him in a singsong voice. Her tone is sickly sweet and I giggle at the look of annoyance on Jeffrey's face.

"Listen up," says Isaac in a whisper only we can hear. "There's just a little bit of time till my mother marches over here."

Jeffrey looks around for her. "Coast is clear," he announces.

"Good. Do you all know who Solly Herschel is?"

"Yes, he's the guy running for the city council from our district, right?" says Hannah.

"That's right. Well, I've been working on his campaign."

Three sets of eyebrows are raised.

"I overheard the men in our synagogue talking about him. They called him an upstart," I tell them.

"Exactly," replies Isaac, grinning. "I think of him as a modern-day prophet, like Isaiah or Jonah, telling the people things they refuse to hear." He gestures in a half-circle with his good arm. "Unlike most people here he's not hiding under a rock ignoring what is as plain as the bandage on my face. He knows they are after us and he thinks we need to begin to defend ourselves and eventually fight back."

Jeffrey holds up both hands. "I'm no fighter. I get what this guy is saying but look around you, Leventhal. Do you really expect a bunch of Orthodox Torah scholars to fight back?"

"You told me your father was in the GFS Army," I respond.

"It was the Air Force, SJ, and he was a mechanic, just like he is now. Not exactly hand-to-hand combat."

"Well, Solly was in the Israeli Army for four years," Isaac says. "He commanded a unit in combat before he came back here."

"I bet he wishes he'd stayed there," Hannah offers.

Isaac shakes his head. "No, he goes where he's needed most."

Again Jeffrey resumes his lookout stance. "The Rebbetzin is headed this way."

Isaac looks up and nods. "Okay, so in the precious seconds remaining, I want us all to meet on Tuesday after school. I'll let you know where. Solly is going to teach the four of us Krav Maga, the Israeli Army's martial arts defense system."

"Isaac!" Jeffrey and I say his name together and turn toward one another. "I don't think—" we both begin, and then smile and sigh with the knowledge that our response is the same.

Isaac stands, walks toward his mother, and turns back to us. "No arguments. We begin to defend ourselves Tuesday. Even though some of us are scared and some of us," he points at his right arm, "are temporarily not at our best. The days of us lying bleeding in the mud while they walk away unharmed are over!"

* * *

Isaac's mention of the Israeli Army makes me think about the Holy Land and the old city of Jerusalem in particular. It's a place that's always fascinated me. A walled city within a modern-day city. A living symbol of the past with four quarters, one for Jews, Muslims, Christians, and Armenians.

I spend all of Saturday night and Sunday working on a papercut of the Damascus Gate, the most beautiful of all of the eight gates with its two imposing turrets and a small bridge leading from the stone plaza to the gate opening.

I know I need to begin thinking about a new design for Jeffrey's next email to Dani, but once the vision of an idea comes to me, I have to make it mine. Besides, I need to know the message that Jeffrey wants to send before I can figure out what the papercut has to include. We've decided it's safe enough to attach a photograph of my art in the email, hoping that anyone who might review it will just think we are sending Dani religious-themed art.

On Monday, Jeffrey meets me at the front of my school looking like he's seen a ghost. His face is pale, even more than usual, and he is a bit bent over staring at the ground instead of looking at me. He jumps when I say his name.

"Is he gone yet?"

"Who?" I ask and look around. There's a bunch of girls from my school standing outside talking, and one rather tall boy who is over by the dreaded Yetta, as Hannah and I have begun to call her.

"You mean the guy over there?"

He looks up quickly and then back down. "Yeah," he breathes.

"Who is he and why is he talking to Yetta?"

"Figures," Jeffrey groans. "Simeon Rausch, a horrible person. Get a look at his soul, SJ. You'll see."

This is the first time Jeffrey has given any credence to the existence of my gift. Up until now, he's treated it like a big joke. I fix my gaze on the large hulking figure with dark hair standing with Yetta, hoping my gift doesn't let me down.

Then I see it. The endless dark tunnel radiating out from him. Without thinking, I gag and a harsh sounding "ugh" comes out of my mouth.

Jeffrey finally lifts his head and turns to me. "Just as I thought," he says. "What did it look like?"

It is so much easier for me to describe the good souls, even the special ones like Jeffrey's and Dvorah's. A malevolent soul is just much more difficult. I do my best to put it into words for Jeffrey. I really want him to believe that I can see into the souls of some people. It's important that he really trust me.

"It's like a dark tunnel," I tell him. "I can see only so far into it, but I have a sense it continues way beyond. His is among the worst I've seen, which is why it made me a bit sick to my stomach."

"Yeah, I know the feeling. What made you feel sick? It wasn't just the tunnel?"

I take another look so I can describe it better, but after a few seconds I have to turn away.

"Greenish-brown creatures, like snakes but not snakes, squirming at the entrance to the tunnel, slime of the same color dripping from them. Not something you'd want to look at for more than a few seconds."

"You know, SJ, I may be growing soft but I actually believe you see something because he is *that* bad."

Our community is not very large, so I'm surprised I haven't seen this Simeon before. He wasn't at the mixer where I met Jeffrey.

"Why haven't I seen him before?" I ask as Jeffrey and I begin our usual walk home.

"Consider yourself lucky. He's a year ahead of us. His family moved here last year from somewhere in Florida that was probably getting a little too wet, if you know what I mean."

The reports of rising sea levels on the coasts reach us from time to time even with the GFS's restrictions on Internet access. Jeffrey read one of Dani's emails to me where she talked about a place called Disneyworld that had moved from Florida to Georgia, but she didn't say why. Jeffrey filled in the blanks for me and said he suspected that some of Florida was either under water or too swampy for anything like an amusement park.

"Has this Simeon been mean to you?"

Jeffrey sighs. "Oh SJ, how do I even begin? If you felt sick looking at his soul, I'm not sure I want to further risk your health or your innocence."

The mention of my so-called innocence rattles me. Most of the time I can deal with Jeffrey's cynicism and sarcastic remarks. But not always his judgments, especially when they relate to me.

I stop walking and he has to backtrack to stand next to me. "What?" he asks.

I stiffen and practically hug myself trying to contain my growing anger at him. "You're not being fair assuming I'm so innocent. You don't know me as well as you think you do,

Jeffrey." I stop before I say something even meaner that I might regret. Even though he's wound me up, he's still a close friend and I care about him.

He sighs. "I'm sorry, Judith, really. It is not easy for me to talk about Simeon Rausch and I guess I tried to come up with a way to avoid it. I know I upset you."

I can hear he's choked up and on the verge of tears. He's back to looking at the ground.

I have no idea how I move from anger to compassion in seconds, but I do. I want to touch his shoulder, to comfort him, but know I cannot. If someone saw us, my parents would find out and we'd be under a *chuppah* the day after my sister Shuli's wedding. I decide instead that it's best to change the subject.

"Are you doing that thing with Isaac tomorrow?" I ask.

I hear him breathe out with what I assume is relief that I've moved on. "Do we have much of a choice? Besides, I'm a bit interested to meet this Solly Herschel, our new savior."

I smile at him. His cynicism is back to being amusing.

"I guess if you and Hannah go, then I'll go."

"We are a quirky but mighty foursome, aren't we SJ?"

I nod and realize he is absolutely right.

"Oh hey," he says, his tone much more upbeat. "I have a new email from Dani and," he turns toward my ear and whispers, "she included a coded message that looks a bit like our code."

I let the reference to "our code" pass even though I think of it as mine and Hannah's, not his. Besides, I'm fascinated by the fact that Dani is now including secret messages to Jeffrey.

"What does she say?"

"I don't know yet. I was hoping we could figure it out together. Can you come to my dad's shop for a bit? There's a newer and more powerful computer there, a Xio4000, one of the best China makes."

"How did your father get a Chinese computer? I thought we can only get GFS machines?"

"I'm not really sure. He bought it from a GFS dealer, but the rest is a mystery I'm not all that interested in unraveling since I'd rather focus on Dani's message."

I'd been in the store once before with my mother who had brought a broken food processor that she needed fixed so she could grate potatoes for Chanukah. When I walk in with Jeffrey this time, I see the same wooden shelves lining three walls, cluttered with all kinds of devices, kitchen appliances, and a variety of screens.

Mr. Schwartz's smile greets us and instantly I worry that once again we are assumed to be a couple. I have no idea how to disabuse anyone of that notion including my own parents.

In any case, Mr. Schwartz is incredibly sweet to me. There is no trace of his son's cynicism.

"Miss Braverman," he says, practically bowing to me, "to what do we owe the pleasure?"

Jeffrey lets out an "Oy" of embarrassment. "Papa, I just want to show Judith something on the computer in the back. We won't be long."

The smile remains on his father's face. "Go *kinder*, I have plenty to do up front. I won't bother you."

I thank him and follow Jeffrey through a doorway into an even more cluttered workroom filled with tables holding pieces of metal and wires of all sizes. There on the back wall, sitting on a metal table, is a very large screen, which I assume to be the fancy computer.

Jeffrey rolls over a second chair and motions for me to sit. "Now, SJ, you will see just why the Chinese are eating our lunch when it comes to technology."

I notice right away that this computer has no keyboard and nothing to control the cursor like the one we have at home. When Jeffrey touches the screen, a keyboard flashes onto the table and he enters a code, and then says "Jeffrey's email" aloud. Instantly a list of his emails appears with the one on the top from Dani highlighted as unread.

"Open," he says, and Dani's message fills the screen.

"Pretty impressive, huh?" he asks turning to me, a big grin on his face. "I enabled the voice recognition utility."

I meet his smile with my own, and nod. His excitement about technology exceeds my own but even though I spend most of my time on a more low-tech art form, I can appreciate how easy and fast this new computer is.

Sitting side by side, we read her email silently.

Dear Jeffrey,

Thank for your last email and for the papercut. Your friend Judith is an artistic genius. I hope she doesn't mind that I shared her work with my project group, a very smart and trustworthy crew. There's Ibi, who is originally from Nigeria and is the editor of our school news site; Aisha, an amazing writer and close friend of mine (I hope you can do the math); Trey, who I've known since I was a baby and is the most ethical person in the world; and Julia, a tech wizard who I think, Jeffrey, you'd just adore as a kindred spirit. Ibi has nicknames for all of us. Here are two of them. I'm "25" because my grandfather is African American (25%, get it?). Julia is "Owl" because her name is pronounced "hoo-lia" like you'd say it in Spanish. So Ibi decided in his twisted mind that hoo-hoo sounded like an owl. Don't ask.

Anyway, I enjoyed learning about the Hebrew words on the papercuts and I thought I'd share some words that my group and I came up with from the Weissberg Torah, Exodus 3:2 and also show you that I can use a Hebrew keyboard and type some letters.

Let me know what you think.

Dani

Jeffrey is so excited he is literally shaking, and for the first time he forgets himself and grabs my arm. "Judith, she's continuing with the code! This is incredible!"

I look at my arm and he lets go as if it was burning his hand. "Sorry," he says.

I spend a second or two thinking about how it felt when he touched me for the first time, and realize it just felt normal, like when Hannah grabs my arm because she sees a new spray-painted anti-Jewish message on the side of a building before they've had a chance to remove it. Jeffrey's touch did not feel any different than when Shuli pulls me away from braiding the challah because I haven't dusted my father's study before Shabbes like I said I would. It all makes me wonder just why this is so forbidden.

Jeffrey has called up the Weissberg Torah on the screen and slides a piece of paper and a pencil in front of me. "Here's Exodus 3:2, SJ, use your superpowers and start decoding."

I follow the code we created. Jeffrey looks over my shoulder as I write down each letter, but when I finish, he grabs hold of the paper and studies it.

"It makes no sense," I tell him. "Maybe I didn't get it right."

"No, SJ, she's sent us another instruction. 'Reply and enter pix.' She wants us to reply to the email and type p-i-x."

It still makes no sense, but I watch as Jeffrey hits reply and types the letters from the keyboard projected onto the table. For a few seconds nothing happens and my thoughts turn to Dani's parenthetical comment, "You do the math." Just as I'm going to ask Jeffrey what he thinks she meant, there's a flash of light from the computer screen and a purple beam comes toward us. I rear back a bit at the suddenness of it and then am confronted with something I can't explain. It's the image of little being, a girl with small wings. She's very thin, dressed in a skimpy one-piece purple outfit. It's sleeveless and only covers the top part of her thighs. She is wearing little purple slippers with a pompom on top of each. Her blond hair is piled on top of her head and she's holding what looks like a thin wand.

"Hi Jeffrey," she says in a high-pitched voice. "I'm Pix, short for Pixie Presto Puff from *The Abby Cadabra Show*. I'm a fairy creature. See my wings?"

Jeffrey and I look at each other. Our eyes are open wide, mouths agape. She begins to speak again.

"I've been sent by Dani so she can speak openly. But first, she wants to make sure you were able to discover me. If you could, when you send the next papercut, please include in it the image of the burning bush so Dani will know I reached you. Oh, and before I go, Dani wants you to know that she and her friends want to help. Please tell them how. Bye for now."

And with a wave of her wand she fades into a purple mist and then the trail of light that brought her seems to retract back into the screen.

Now it is me who is trembling. I've seen souls, both good and bad. I've heard prophesies and have befriended one of the righteous thirty-six, but even so, this being, this Pix, defies any explanation.

"A hologram," Jeffrey whispers. "Dani must know how to make them."

"A what?"

"It's a special light field that creates a three-dimensional image. She mentioned in one of her emails that she was learning about them. She must have the technology to be able to create one and to hide it in an email."

He is shaking his head at the screen in amazement. "This is even better than our code."

"No," I say as it dawns on me. "She needs to use our code to tell us how to unlock this Pix thing. They work together."

"Yes," he says. "You're right. I wish we could create our own little Pix. I wonder what kind of creature I'd want to use."

Jeffrey is leaning on his elbow, positioned next to the projected keyboard, his head resting on his open hand. Our minds are going in different directions. I'm certain his is filled with all kinds of technical thoughts while I'm wondering about Dani's words—"You do the math"—and Pix's message that she's from something called Abby Cadabra and that Dani and her friends want to help us.

I see the search box on the computer screen and am astounded when I can type my question by tapping on the image of the keyboard. "Who is Abby Cadabra?" I ask the computer.

Jeffrey looks at the screen and I hear him chuckle. "After everything we just saw and heard, that's the question you have, SJ?"

"Don't you want to know where that creature comes from and who she is?"

"She comes from Dani Fine. That's all I need to know."

I ignore him and read the words that appear on the screen. *Abby Cadabra* is the name of a book, a film, and a cartoon series. Abby is the main character, the child of magicians who one day made themselves disappear and never came back. I scroll down using my finger, looking for the name Pix, and then I see Pixie Presto Puff, the full name the creature used. And just as she told us, she's a fairy in that story who comes to life when children say, "Fairies bring the light."

I try it, wondering if maybe she will come back. "Fairies bring the light. Fairies bring the light."

Jeffrey is laughing, his hand covering his mouth. "You really think that is going to bring her back? She's a product of technology, not magic."

I feel my cheeks warm. He's right of course. But after all I've seen and been able to see, plus this newest vision, I'm having difficulty distinguishing between reality and magic and gifts and all the rest.

"Listen, Judith." Jeffrey is suddenly serious. "I need to tell you something." Because he is looking everywhere but at me, I figure that whatever this is it must be difficult.

"Okay," I respond, keeping my voice soft, "go ahead."

He says the words quickly without pausing for breath. They run into one another. "I'm just like Pix, like she said, she's a fairy, well I'm a fairy too, or as we say here in our little intolerant community, I'm a *fagele*, which is why I need to leave the GFS and defect to the UPR." He finally takes a breath, and then blurts out, "In case you need it spelled out for you even more, Judith, I like boys, not girls. I'm gay."

I stare at him though he still won't look at me. Jeffrey, my friend, the person closest to me after Hannah. A boy who never asked for more than what I wanted to give. In that moment, I understand both everything and nothing of what he has told me. And I have no idea what to do with this information. Words seem inadequate, and even if they weren't, I have no idea what the right ones would be.

So in spite of everything I've been taught, in spite of Mr. Schwartz working on the other side of the door, I lean over and pull him to my chest. He collapses into me and he's sobbing.

"Shaaa," I whisper in his ear. "It's okay." And then I say the craziest thing that comes into my mind, "You heard me. I said you bring the light."

CHAPTER THIRTEEN

Dani

Julia and I are standing in our group room looking at the projection of Jeffrey's latest email and his photo of the new papercut.

Julia points to the image of a burning bush in the photo. "So he unlocked Pix," she says.

I look at the small bush and can spot some short branches and leaves. But what's most prominent are the flames, shooting skyward. Judith has used orange paper as her backing, but the papercut itself is off-white. Once again I marvel at her talent and wonder how we might combine our artforms one day. Holograms and papercuts—could we find some way to put them together?

I say none of what I'm thinking and only reply, "Yeah it worked."

She turns to me. Her broad face breaks into a smile. "I'm glad you decided to go with Pix instead of Anne Frank, Dani."

Trey, seated near us looking at something on a white board, must have heard her. "Agreed, babe," they call out to their girlfriend. "Jeffrey and Judith have enough drama going on down there without being reminded of the Holocaust."

They're right, of course, but even so it had been hard to let go of Anne Frank. She'd been my first idea for the hologram because I thought they would know who she was, and because I'm a bit obsessed with her and with the Holocaust.

I read her diary when I was twelve and then read everything I could find about the rise of National Socialism in Germany and the worsening persecution of Jews, Roma, and queers. I read novels like *Exodus* and the memoirs of Elie Wiesel and Primo Levi. One night while I was lying in bed reading about the women's camp, Ravensbruck, my mother came in and point-blank asked me what this was all about, this fixation, as she called it.

At first I didn't know how to respond. I hadn't really thought about the reason. I just followed my interest, like someone with a fascination about any historical event. It could've easily been the USA Civil War or The Split.

But my mother wasn't buying it. "This is too much of a troubling horror for you to be so immersed, Dani. Do you have any thought about what's behind it?"

I insisted that my interest was just that, an interest, and sent my mother away so I could keep reading. But her question stayed with me, even though I could never hit on an answer.

Then one day when my dad announced at dinner that Binyamin would be visiting in two weeks, I had a breakthrough. As always, the mention of my brother got me thinking about his life in the GFS. He was living there as an Orthodox Jew because he'd been promised religious freedom; and I knew how difficult it would be for Binyamin and his family to live as Orthodox Jews here in the UPR. There are synagogues in Columbus, but none like the ones they are used to, and certainly no rabbis like those they have. Because his religion is so important to him and to Miriam, I kind of understand his decision to live in the south.

But recently, from what he's been telling us when he visits, it's starting to look like he's living among people who would prefer he and the rest of the Jews live somewhere else. Isn't that how all the books describe the way it started long ago in Germany? The people among you might tolerate you, but when it came down to it, they would rather you not be in their midst.

Suddenly my appetite was gone, and I told my parents I wasn't in the mood to eat. Instead I walked out to the backyard and sat on one of the redwood Adirondack chairs on our deck. The sun was low, casting long shadows of the chairs and the red maple in our yard. I rested my feet on the deck's wooden railing and thought about my brother.

As my father raised the subject of Binyamin's visit at dinner, I realized that it was my brother and his little family who were at the root of my so-called Holocaust fixation. I needed to understand how it had all gone down before so that I could… what? Be ready for it this time? Warn Binyamin? I wasn't sure.

The day after my realization I asked Kat to find me a new book about the Holocaust, something I had not come across before. Surely there had to be something about Jews doing more than surviving the camps and the ghettos. Not that survival wasn't a form of resistance, but I wanted more. I wanted to know about the Jews who had resisted when no one else would come to their aid. And Kat found it—an anthology called *They Fought Back: The Story of the Jewish Resistance in Nazi Europe*. I read and reread it. It became my go-to book on the subject. Resistance cells. Partisans fighting in the forests, blowing up railroad tracks. Women working in munitions factories sabotaging weapons.

It gave me hope that there could be a way for Binyamin, his family, and also Jeffrey and Judith, to fight back.

As I told Jeffrey in my last email, Julia is a computer whiz and I knew she'd be able to write some kind of little program that would instantly decode the message behind the Hebrew letters in Judith's papercuts.

Now, with the burning bush projected in front of us, I stand watching as Julia uses her iBrain to take a screenshot of the Hebrew letters Judith cut into the picture.

"The program will read these, find the exact place in the Weissberg Torah and decode the message," she explains. "At least I hope it will."

Again, Trey offers their opinion. "Of course it will, babe. You're a genius."

These two are the most annoyingly adoring couple in the world, and I love them both. Trey and I were babies in the same playgroup way back when. It was clear pretty early that Trey was rejecting any efforts to conform to the gender they'd been assigned at birth. So their parents did what any good parent in the UPR did when they realized they had a gender nonconforming child. Trey was on hormone blockers so they wouldn't develop into a female adolescent, and then went about the journey of transitioning ending up as a somewhat masculine nonbinary. Luckily, Trey was their given name, so all the rest of us had to do was change the pronoun.

For Julia, it was a bit more difficult. Her parents weren't thrilled that the child they thought was their son was actually a daughter. It was her *abuela* who saved the day and took charge of Julia's transition, bringing her parents along slowly.

To Ibi, Julia and Trey are simply, the couple. Whenever he wants their attention, he'll call out something like, "Can the couple please come talk to me." It's just another of his nicknames that we put up with, though it's interesting that none of us have figured out the best way to refer to him.

I stand impatiently next to Julia who is running the program on her device, silently communicating with her iBrain which is in turn filling her head with information I won't have access to until she tells me. My body is moving back and forth, my arms swaying with it. I try marching in place.

"Dani, calm it already," says Trey through their laughter.

I turn and stick my tongue out at them and they respond in kind. But our childish exchange is interrupted by Julia.

"Oh wow," she says. "This changes everything." Her hand is over her mouth as she stares at the projected photo of the papercut.

I grab hold of her, desperate to know the message that she has already read. She points to a white board and it appears.

RABBI'S SON ATTACKED BY THUGS. JS IS GAY. NEEDS TO LEAVE. HELP.

I stand there paralyzed, except for the words "Oh no, oh no" that keep coming out of my mouth. Trey walks over to where Julia and I are standing. Even Ibi and Aisha leave their little fiefdoms, as we call their work areas, and join us.

Jeffrey Schwartz is gay. What are the odds that I would end up with a gay pen pal? Could Binyamin or his sister-in-law have arranged this? Doubtful.

"We have to get him out of there. They'll kill him," Aisha says.

"Or send him to one of those conversion camps," adds Trey.

"You mean concentration camps," Julia responds.

"One way or another, he'll be dead. His body, his spirit or both." That's Aisha again.

This is not a crowd that holds back, and when it comes to the GFS they always assume the worst. I'm usually the dissenter among them, mostly out of allegiance to my brother. Because, while I'm not religious, I always defend Binyamin's right to be, especially given my mother's never-ending campaign to change him.

Except now. Given Binyamin's latest reports of violence and the coded messages I've received from Jeffrey, I'm starting to side with my friends' opinions about the GFS, and more importantly I'm worried about my brother and his family.

I think about all the Jewish women in the Holocaust I've read about. Anne Frank hid and was discovered. She was transported on the very last train the Nazis sent from Holland to Auschwitz. Hannah Arendt and many other famous Jews were able to leave and come to the USA. Roza Robota helped smuggle explosives from a concentration camp factory that were used in a prisoner revolt. She and four other women were hanged by the Nazis. Ruzka Korczak left the Vilna ghetto and became a member of the Avengers, a group of partisans who engaged in sabotage and guerrilla attacks against the Nazis. She survived the war and died in 1988.

Then there was Hannah Senesh, an Israeli who risked and lost her life when she parachuted into Hungary to try to prevent the transport of Jews. She was captured and tortured but refused to divulge any of the details of her mission.

As I stand there surrounded by the friends closest to me, I can't help but wonder who would I be in the face of such horrors? Who are Jeffrey, Judith, and Binyamin? And given what may be happening in the south, who do we all now need to be?

Aisha tugs on my shoulders and pulls me into a hug. We are no longer together, but the fact that we were, and now remain friends, means that we have fewer physical boundaries than I might have with other people. The beads on her braids tickle my nose and I smell her pleasant musky lemon skin cream. Even though she is a self-described warrior, there's also a softness to her that she lets me see. I wonder if that's true for any of her current girlfriends, however many of them there are these days.

"Your father," she says when we end the hug. "Can he help get Jeffrey across the border?"

"I don't know. It's not so easy, and it could get him in trouble."

"But isn't he in charge of the entire Ohio border?" she asks.

I've overhead my mother begging him to smuggle my brother and his family into North Ohio, even though my brother wants to stay where he is. Her pleas always lead to the same explanation from my dad. While there is no visible barrier between the two countries, there are laser guardrails and video monitors everywhere, not all controlled by the UPR.

So even if we wanted to get Jeffrey across, I'm not sure we could, and the asylum process is also not easy. As soon as Jeffrey's application was submitted to his government, he'd become a pariah in the GFS. And the reason for his request, the fact that he's gay, would become public knowledge.

But as I stand there ready to tell this to Aisha, I realize it all must have seemed futile to Ruzka Korczak during World War II as she and her fellow partisans hid in the woods planning to fight a well-armed enemy with only rifles and a few explosives. But she and they kept going in spite of that, hoping to find a way to hit back, and celebrating each little victory.

I nod at Aisha, resolved to figure out how we can do something to help Jeffrey, even though I have no idea what it could be.

CHAPTER FOURTEEN

Jeffrey

I've paid close attention to Judith these past few weeks, ready for any sign that things are different now that she knows about me. But to my utter relief, she seems fine. We still walk home from school together. She still teases me when I call her SJ, and our little quartet, with Isaac and Hannah, seems to be going strong.

Judith promised she wouldn't tell anyone, but begged me to let her talk to Dvorah Kuriel of all people. Sure, the great rabbi's daughter. Why not just take out a full-page ad in Judith's father's newspaper: *Jeffrey Schwartz is a fagele. Have at him.*

But she assures me that Dvorah is both trustworthy and openminded. Apparently they have met several times and, as Judith tells me, they both have these magical gifts. Judith can see souls (which maybe I'm starting to believe a little bit) and Dvorah can tell us the future.

"Only in broad outlines," Judith explains. As if that clears everything up.

So today, after our weekly Krav Maga lesson with Solly Herschel, Judith and I are having afternoon tea at Dvorah's. I roll my eyes. In spite of any stereotypes about those with my sexual proclivities, I am not an afternoon tea kind of guy.

"So SJ, which pinky do I have to extend when I lift the cup?" I ask her.

She lets out a breath and shakes her head. "You're impossible. It's not like that at all. You drink the tea, eat the rugelach and talk to her. That's it."

"Ummm, rugelach, why didn't you mention that before?"

"Mama always says that a way to a man's heart is through his stomach. Maybe she's right?"

"Well, while I think the world of you SJ, the truth is I can only give you so much of my heart and no more," I say as I open the door to Solly's campaign office where we take our Krav Maga lessons.

I change into the T-shirt and sweatpants that Solly keeps for us on a shelf in the back room of his campaign office where the walls are lined with cardboard boxes and a thick blue mat is laid out in the middle of the floor. As I'm pushing my arms through the sleeves of my T-shirt, it occurs to me that Judith has never given me a moment's worry about wanting more from me than friendship. And in all the time we've spent together, I've never asked her about her own romantic inclinations. Does she get crushes on boys? Is she a late bloomer?

In his own way, Solly Herschel is as yummy to look at as Isaac. Unlike the slim and handsome rabbi's son, Solly is built a bit like a tank, broader than tall, arms like the kind of clubs that cavemen carried, and short legs that make me think of tree trunks. His dark hair is cut close to his head and, unlike Isaac, he does sport a beard. Believe me, if you came across a guy who looked like him in a dark alley, you'd be whispering the *Sh'ma* prayer thinking you were about to meet your end. But if the alley was all lit up, you'd relax when you saw Solly's broad smile and his bright dark eyes that actually do twinkle.

Isaac is still working on Solly's campaign, though he can't be out holding signs or going door to door. The rabbi would go nuts. So it's Hannah who has risked the wrath of her parents and is out there in front of the kosher bakery on Thursdays after school, passing out handbills to the women shopping for Shabbes. Even

Judith has agreed to design posters and campaign leaflets, that is, after I give her a quick lesson in desktop publishing.

Today is our fourth Krav Maga class and the last one before Isaac gets the cast removed. I watch as he scratches around it and pray silently that I never break a limb and have to wear a cast. Of course everyone at school has signed it, and Judith drew a beautiful picture of Judah Maccabee, the leader who led a revolt against one of the many oppressors of the Jews and restored the Temple in Jerusalem so we could have Hanukkah. Or something to that effect. I don't always listen in Jewish History class. In any case, the picture was pretty cool and Isaac said he's keeping that part of the cast because Judith might be a famous artist one day and it might be worth something.

We're finally learning some physical moves from Solly after spending the first few lessons listening to him explain the philosophy behind Krav Maga (defend and attack was what I took from it) and the principle of situational awareness (looking for escape routes, other attackers, or objects you could use to fight back). I liked the idea of an escape route, but as Isaac said when I mentioned it, if there's three goons coming at you, you'd better learn how to fight back.

Since Isaac is still unable to do the physical stuff, Solly wants me to be the one standing on the floor mat fending off his attack. While most guys would be offended to be shown up by a girl, I am not most guys, and I breathe an enormous sigh of relief when Hannah gets up and offers to take my place. Go Hannah.

Judith looks appalled and gives me the side-eye, but I ignore her. After all, there's four of us in the class. So what if Hannah goes first.

Isaac is spellbound, like he is with most things when it comes to Hannah. He can't keep his eyes off her. She actually gets to a point after about ten minutes of practice with Solly where she can pull away the stick he's holding as a weapon, turn his body and push it against the wall.

"Well done, Hannah! *Yasher koach*," announces Solly, and the three of us applaud. "Okay, Jeffrey, up on your feet *boychick*."

Judith will not go next and save me. I am sure of that. So I slowly stand, approach Solly and hold out my hand like I want to shake his in greeting. "Hi?" I say, and everyone laughs.

"Isaac," he says, "why don't you stand here for moral support?" Solly points to a place on the floor that's about five feet beyond where I am on the mat. I'm not sure if Isaac is the best choice for moral support since he's such a major distraction for me. I would have chosen Judith. But I decide to trust Solly's judgment.

He is teaching me how to deflect an attack and turn things around so that I am the aggressor. Good luck with that.

This time he doesn't use a weapon. Instead he shows me how to grab the arm he's about to use to punch my stomach, then knee him in the gut and twist his body so he falls flat on his back. We work on the kneeing part first.

"Harder, Jeffrey," he says. "Use all your strength. I'll be fine."

He's such a nice guy, it doesn't feel right to hurt him. But when I hesitate, it's me who lands on my back. I will admit to not having a lot of self-respect, but I do have enough not to spend the next ten minutes getting thrown about like a ragdoll. So I knee him hard and manage somehow to twist his body. He doesn't fall but the fact that I've gotten this far is a bit of a triumph. I'll take it.

When it's her turn, Judith is taught how to pull a gun away from an attacker even when it's pointed right at her little forehead. It takes her a bunch of tries, but she finally gets it and we applaud.

It's more than enough for one day and I'm thrilled to put my regular clothes back on even if the next stop on our itinerary is Dvorah Kuriel's teahouse.

But there's yet another surprise in store for us before we get there. The front room of Solly's campaign office is crowded with desks and chairs, with campaign signs and a large map of the neighborhood tacked to one of the gray walls. There are flyers, files, and pads of paper piled high on every surface. Amid all of this clutter, I spot Professor Fine and his little son Yuval, who's about ten. The professor is holding a clipboard and is looking up at the map and then down at something he is writing. I walk in their direction, wave Judith over and clear my throat. By the look on his face, he is surprised to see us, but his raised eyebrows give way to a smile.

"Jeffrey, Judith, are you helping out here too?"

I nod and the professor and I shake hands while Judith talks to Yuval, asking him about his brother and sister. It seems that Professor Fine has taken charge of Solly's field operation.

"This guy," he says, placing his hand on Solly's shoulder, "is going to make a big difference for us. So we need to do everything we can to get him elected."

Hannah and Isaac remain with Solly to help with a mailing and Judith and I leave for our next appointment.

"Were you surprised to see Professor Fine there?" she asks once we leave the office.

"At first yes, but then when I thought about it, I remembered he agreed with me about the president's daughter and was pretty clear when he spoke to my class that we had to take to heart the lessons of Germany in the nineteen thirties. So it makes sense that he's working for Solly."

We walk in silence until we are almost there, and then Judith turns to me.

"The house," she says and points down the block, "is not at all what I expected when I first went there. I guess I thought someone like Rabbi Kuriel would live in a palace. But it's a very modest home, kind of minimal inside and very clean and orderly, nothing like my house."

"Or my father's shop."

I stop walking. "You know, I've never been to a rabbi's house before."

"It's okay, really. Dvorah'll make you feel comfortable immediately."

"Will she tell my fortune?" I whisper this next part. "I want to know if I'm ever going to get a boyfriend?"

It's hard to describe the look on Judith's face for a few seconds. Maybe she's surprised that I actually said the word out loud, though she's not exactly registering surprise. It's more like a serious look, like her wheels are turning and she's determined not to react. But then there's a little smile. A small upturn of the mouth that I recognize by now as a show of affection for me.

I wave her off. "Okay, okay. I know she's not a miracle worker, SJ."

Inside the Kuriel house I'm not feeling as immediately comfortable as Judith predicted. This Dvorah is an imposing woman. I don't need to see her soul to know that. But she does seem incredibly happy to meet me for some reason. I hope she hasn't pegged me as Judith's intended husband because she'll be sorely disappointed. She makes good on the rugelach. I will give her that. There's even chocolate, my favorite kind.

Judith tells her about our Krav Maga instruction, and I worry that my friend is too trusting of this woman. But Dvorah seems pleased to hear about it. Like Solly, her now deceased husband was once in the Israeli Army and was also skilled in this Jewish version of martial arts.

And if that isn't enough spilling of the proverbial beans, I sit there in shock when Judith asks Dvorah whether I should leave the GFS.

Dvorah sits quietly for a few seconds and then nods her head in thought. "Times are getting harder. And likely will get worse. There's no doubt about that. Is this something your family is considering, Jeffrey?"

"Ah no," I squeak out. "Just me." I'm not yet able to speak to her easily.

Judith has no such trouble apparently. She takes a gulp of her tea, places the cup on its saucer and spills my life all over the table.

"It's not just that Jeffrey is Jewish like all of us," she says. "He's also gay."

I literally hold my breath waiting for the reaction.

Dvorah nods, again lost in thought. "Yes, that does make your life more difficult." She stands and motions for us to follow her into another room.

She arranges some chairs in front of a screen that sits atop a small table and types a few keys on a keyboard. The screen comes to life and there is a black and white picture of a young man on a playing field. He's handsome and athletic-looking.

"I want to share the lives of some of our people with the both of you. Have you ever heard of Fredy Hirsch?"

Judith and I look at each other, thinking maybe the other one has. But we both shrug.

"Well," Dvorah continues, "that doesn't surprise me. They won't teach you about him in school. Fredy Hirsch was a young German Jew and a hero of the Shoah. You see him here on the playing field as the athletic instructor of Jewish children. In the Theresienstadt ghetto and even in Auschwitz, Fredy organized activities for children, both athletic and otherwise. He insisted on strict hygiene to keep them healthy. While not all of the children under his care survived, the ones who did credit him with saving their lives."

Interesting story I think, but why are we hearing this?

"So why tell you about Fredy Hirsch?" Dvorah asks as if she can read my thoughts, which given who she is, is entirely possible. "Well, Fredy was not only Jewish, he was also gay, and openly so. This was at a time like ours when it was not looked upon kindly. But to the people he cared for, he was a *tzadik*, one of the righteous thirty-six. I don't know if that was the case, only Hashem knows for sure, but he was a gay Jewish hero."

Judith and I sit there amazed, our mouths open. Dvorah sees us and smiles.

"Okay," she says, "let's move on to the next one."

Another black and white photo appears of a man in a jacket and tie. Clearly Jewish, I can tell from the dark hair and the prominent nose.

"Harvey Milk, a Jewish politician and the first openly gay man to win election in the USA back in 1977. He inspired thousands of young people to live open lives."

She clicks on the keyboard and the next picture appears. It's a handsome older man with graying hair and a short graying beard. Wire rim glasses and prominent nose complete the picture. Then I notice it. He's wearing a yarmulke.

"This is the last one I will show you, though we could be here all day since there are so many." She looks pointedly at Judith. "Women too, though today for Jeffrey's benefit we are focusing on the men. This is Rabbi Steven Greenberg. That's right, I said rabbi. In 1999, he became the first Orthodox rabbi to declare himself publicly as gay and went on to teach and help many other Orthodox Jewish gay people."

She shuts down the computer and beckons us back into the kitchen. Once we are seated and I have an entire chocolate rugelach filling my mouth, she holds out both her arms, palms open, as if gathering us to her.

"I hope you now know that there is a legacy of pioneering and heroic Jewish gay men from whom you can draw strength, Jeffrey. These are people who rose above the difficulties of their times and inspired many others. Who knows how many lives they saved?"

Judith is looking at me as if she's expecting something. But I don't know what. A reaction? A show of appreciation? A determination to become a hero? Which I am not!

I fold into myself. My back is flush with the chair, my arms crossed over my chest. *What do you all want from me?*

Luckily, Dvorah gives me an out.

"This is a lot to take in, Jeffrey. I can tell you are overwhelmed, which is what I expected. But I also think you will digest all of this and it will help as you consider your decision about whether to stay or to leave. I cannot tell you what to do, of course. I can only help you see some things a little more clearly."

Right now I am as far from clarity as I can be. The three men Dvorah talked about might as well be planets in a distant solar system. Yet, it's hard to ignore the fact that Fredy Hirsch lived at a time that was even more dangerous than mine and still refused to hide who he was. But the thing is, I'm just not that brave of a guy. Not when I can easily wind up even worse than Isaac bleeding to death on the street.

The only way I can ever be myself is to leave. But now with SJ and Isaac and everyone else, I'd be leaving them too.

Judith and I are quiet on our walk home. I'm pretty sure she's letting me digest what I've heard, as Dvorah suggested. But as much as I would like it to be, I am not facing a choice about whether it's better to digest an onion bagel or a bialy. No, it's more like choosing Mercury or Mars.

CHAPTER FIFTEEN

Judith

In her flowing white dress, complete with long train and veil, Shuli is a beautiful bride. David the groom cannot stop smiling that their day is finally here. They stand together in the sanctuary of our synagogue under the wedding canopy, the *chuppah*, reciting their vows of forever. The flowers placed on either side of the *chuppah* match perfectly with my sister's wedding colors, lilac and ivory. Every once in a while I get a whiff of their sweet, heady aroma.

I sit with my mother, my younger sister and our little brother on a padded bench. watching our big sister marry. The men and older boys are seated together across the aisle from us.

After today Shuli will no longer live with us, though she won't be far. My big sister has been a buffer for me when Mama nags me about boys. "Let me take care of her," Shuli says as she ushers me out of the room and then reassures me that "Mama just wants the best for you but she can be a little much. Don't worry, your day will come."

I will now have Shuli's assigned chores to do while not all of mine will be passed on to Leah, my younger sister. That means busier Friday afternoons and less time braiding challah.

Downstairs in the large social hall, the reception food table is overflowing with everything imaginable. Shuli wanted a *milchig* meal and she and my mother fought about this endlessly.

"The guests will expect brisket," she argued.

But in the end she gave in to my sister and we now have a dozen varieties of fish, four different kugels (potato and noodle) and of course all of the sweets. No one looks disappointed.

I am thankful that the reception seating is not separate for men and women, although the dancing will not be mixed. I managed to get Jeffrey invited though it was at the cost of a look from my mother and the question that followed, which was not really a question, "So you and this boy?"

Given my father's position as publisher of the local paper, most leaders in the community are here, including Professor Fine and his family, as well as Rabbi Leventhal, the Rebbetzin and their six children.

I'm not sure how long my mother will let me sit with my friends, but I grab a free table for four off to the side. One by one, Hannah, Isaac, and Jeffrey find me.

Hannah looks at the two plates piled with food that Jeffrey sets down. "Are you really going to eat all that?"

He pulls the plates closer to him. "Yes. This is the food of the gods, if you'll excuse the expression. SJ, tell your sister I wholeheartedly approve of her menu choices."

I shake my head. "I'm sure she'll be thrilled."

"Look at this little group right here, Ruchel." It's my aunt Pearl and my mother. "You'd better start saving up for the next wedding, huh?"

"Judith, who is this nice young man?" she asks, pointing to Jeffrey.

They have trapped me and there's nothing I can do. I smile and hope I can get my point across. "This is my *friend*, Jeffrey Schwartz," I say, trying to place considerable emphasis on friend. "Jeffrey, this is my aunt Pearl."

Jeffrey is not always the most well-mannered, but he knows enough to stand and acknowledge my aunt. "Nice to meet you," he mumbles. "And congratulations, Mrs. Braverman."

My aunt turns to my mother. "He's a little shy one, isn't he?" It's as if none of us are right there. I notice Hannah has her hand over her mouth to hide her amusement.

"Isaac, it is an honor to have your entire family here on this happy day." My mother apparently feels the need to butter up the rabbi's son since everyone expects that he will one day take his father's place.

Like Jeffrey, Isaac stands, but his congratulations to my mother and his greeting to my aunt are warm and gracious.

"Ah, such a gentleman," my aunt tells my mother. "One day he is certain to make his father proud."

Then she turns to us and drops a bomb. "And have the four of you heard that two of your schoolmates have announced their engagement? Yetta Freundlich will soon marry Simeon Rausch. She's not waiting for graduation, she's so happy."

We are all struck dumb by the news. Simeon with his snake-like soul and the dreaded Yetta are joining forces. Jeffrey looks positively sick to his stomach. He pushes his two plates away. I realize they will think it strange that we do not share their joy, so I offer a nod and a very weak, "How nice for them."

And if all of that wasn't enough, as they prepare to leave us, my aunt feels the need to get one more plea aimed in my direction. Gesturing between me and Jeffrey, she practically gushes, "Judith, may it be God's will that soon I dance at your wedding."

"*Baruch Hashem*," my mother adds, and they are gone.

Jeffrey has folded into what I refer to as his cocoon position, in which he makes himself as small as possible, his arms crossed, his head down. I want to reassure him that it's going to be okay, but I can't deny that the news about Yetta and Simeon is depressing and the pressure is mounting to marry me off, with him as the lucky candidate.

We are all quiet for a minute until Hannah breaks the silence. "Am I invisible?" she asks. "They didn't even acknowledge the fact that I'm sitting right here."

"Consider yourself lucky," says Jeffrey.

"You're never invisible to me," Isaac responds and the look of adoration on his face tells me that if anyone has to start saving for a wedding it's Hannah's parents.

The small band strikes the opening notes of the Hora and two circles, one of men, one of women, are forming.

"Let's leave behind all of this awfulness and go dance," Hannah urges us.

As always, some of the women and girls in my circle know the actual steps of the Hora, while others are happy to just be dragged along in the merriment. Soon both circles are opened, and Shuli and David are hoisted up on chairs carried by young men. David removes a handkerchief from his pocket, and waves it at his bride, who grabs the end so the two are now connected. We all stand laughing and clapping to the music until they are each set down and the two circles re-close. Two young women walk to the middle and swing each other around by their interlocked arms. I wait my turn and do the same with Hannah.

When I look over at the men, I see Jeffrey and Isaac crouched down with knees bent, arms crossed, their feet moving rapidly to the music as they dance around one another. The women stop and watch them and everyone is clapping and cheering.

It occurs to me in that moment that had so many things been different, Isaac would have been a wonderful boyfriend for Jeffrey, and I wonder if Jeffrey thinks the same.

As the various traditions and ceremonies are winding down and people are starting to leave, Jeffrey rushes over to me breathless. "She's here!" he exclaims. "I just saw her." He motions me to come with him. "Quick before she leaves."

He's walking fast, turning back waving his arms to keep me moving. I finally catch up to him and ask, "Who are you talking about?"

"Dvorah Kuriel, of course." As if I was supposed to know all along. "I need to ask her something and I need you with me."

I'm guessing that Dvorah is still too intimidating for him to approach on his own, so we rush over to the other side of the reception hall as she is slipping an arm into a cardigan sweater. She notices us and smiles.

"Why hello there. I'm glad I saw the two of you before I left. My congratulations to your family, Judith, on this happy occasion."

Jeffrey is breathing hard from exertion, but he still manages to blurt out, "Miss, uh, Mrs. uh Kuriel…"

"Please Jeffrey, Dvorah is fine."

"Okay," he exhales. "Dvorah, I have one question about Fredy."

So she was right. He has been thinking about this.

Dvorah nods for him to go ahead.

"Did he ever have the chance to leave Germany?"

There is hardly a second between his question and her reply. "Yes. He'd moved to Czechoslovakia after the Nazis came to power in Germany, but when they took over that country in nineteen thirty-eight, he could have emigrated to Bolivia with his mother and brother where both survived the war. He chose instead to remain with the children under his care."

Dvorah and I watch Jeffrey as he takes this in.

"Let me see what other material I can find for you to learn more about Fredy Hirsch, Jeffrey. It is important to keep his memory alive."

"Yes," he responds. "I'd appreciate that. I'd like to understand more about why he did what he did."

* * *

It's the Monday after the wedding and Jeffrey and I are walking away from my school building. "There's a new message from Dani that I'm waiting to read with you," he says.

Again, Jeffrey approached me with his eyes fixed on the ground in front of him. We've just passed Simeon and Yetta surrounded by a crowd of well-wishers. What could it be about Simeon that prompts such a reaction from him?

"Do you think we'll have another message from Pix?" I ask.

"I hope so."

"Jeffrey, before we read Dani's email, will you please tell me what it is that gets you so worked up when you see Simeon?"

He sighs. "I guess I can tell you, but we need to figure out where. Out here feels too exposed and I don't want to talk about it in my father's workshop."

"I think I know a place," I tell him.

We walk a few blocks and then I head over toward a small red brick building.

"The *mikvah*, SJ? You're joking, right? I can't go in there."

I giggle in response. "We're not going to the *mikvah*, *boychick*. Just come with me."

There's an old corrugated iron shed behind the *mikvah* building that used to be storage for all kinds of extra supplies and fixtures. It hasn't been used in a long time and the iron door is a bit rusted but it still opens. There are a few boxes against the back wall and some random plastic pipes lying on the floor. I sit on a box and Jeffrey does the same.

"How do you know about this place?"

"Hannah and I found it when she first started taking pictures of the graffiti and vandalism. We come here to look at her stuff before she hides it."

"And no one has ever come in here?" he asks.

"No. Which is why I thought it would be a safe place to talk."

He's looking down again. I wish I could cure him of this habit. "All right." He pauses. "So, Simeon."

I decide to wait him out. Whatever this is doesn't seem easy for him and I worry that if I push too hard he won't talk.

"You see, um, the thing is, he did, uh, does, something bad. To me." More pausing and then finally. "He forces himself." He whispers the last two words, "On me."

"He?" I hesitate as the full meaning of his words hit me.

Jeffrey is crouched over the side of the box and he's crying, nodding, and rocking. "Yes," he says through his tears.

"More than once?"

More nodding and rocking.

All I can think is *But he's marrying Yetta*.

"It's so confusing, Judith!" he practically shouts. "It's not how I pictured, you know, but still…Oh God, I can't believe I'm telling you this!"

This is so painful for him that I'm beginning to regret I made him tell me. He's already opened up so much—and what have I done? Made him miserable. And with nothing quite so intimate or hurtful to share in return.

At this point we have obliterated any physical boundaries of propriety that once prevented us from touching. So for the second time I pull him into a hug and let him cry.

After a few minutes, I venture a question. "Is there anyone you can tell? The principal? The rabbi? Your father?"

"No, no, no," he says into my shoulder. "He will leave school and it will stop. I can't risk anyone else knowing about me. I'm not courageous like Fredy Hirsch or Harvey Milk or even that gay rabbi."

As I think about those three heroes Dvorah told us about and wonder what any of them would do, something else suddenly comes to me and I can't keep the excitement out of my voice.

"Jeffrey, you can stop him yourself now."

He pulls back from me and wipes his eyes with his sleeve. "What? How?"

"With the Krav Maga. Last time we had a lesson you were able to stop Solly's attack and push him against the wall."

He's quiet for a few seconds and goes back to sitting on the other box. "I was, wasn't I?"

"You don't have to be Fredy or Harvey or Steven. Dvorah said they were just inspiration so you can know you aren't destined to suffer or be alone. What I think she was trying to tell you is you can be you and that will be enough."

Jeffrey's revelation in the iron shed has exhausted the both of us, even if it ended on a more positive note. We agree that we should wait until the next day to read Dani's email.

Twenty-four hours later, as we walk past Yetta and Simeon, Jeffrey stands up straight and even smiles. It hasn't been pleasant for either of us to be that close to Simeon. I still see glimpses of his sickening soul when I look over at him. When Jeffrey notices my reaction, he shakes his finger at me.

"Why do you put yourself through this, SJ? Haven't you had enough of those disgusting snakes?"

I stop myself from correcting him that the oozing creatures aren't exactly snakes, and instead tell him he's right and anyway we have better things to do.

The fancy computer in Jeffrey's father's workshop once again delivers Dani's email to us.

Dear Jeffrey,

Thanks so much for the beautiful papercut, especially the burning bush. It is always exciting to see Judith's newest creation. I hope you'll tell me more about other friends of yours. My friends and I were glad to hear from you and to learn more about you.

Jeffrey turns to me, his voice filled with anxiety. "Do you think she told them about me?" He drops his head into his hands. "Now everyone in the UPR knows too?"

I put my hand on his shoulder and gently tug so he'll lift his head. "I'm sure it's all right. Let me keep reading."

It seems you and I and some of my friends have much in common and it would be so great to actually meet you. Until then, I leave you with my suggestion that you return to Exodus, but this time you read about the parting of the Red Sea (Exodus 14:15). And I think my Hebrew is improving. What do you think of this?

Dani

The Hebrew letters she included along with the Torah portion help us figure out what we need to do to bring up the hologram. Pix comes streaming forward, this time all dressed in green.

"Greetings Jeffrey and Judith. In case Dani's email was not completely clear, she wants you to know she too is queer as are some of her friends. So Jeffrey, you are not alone."

"Queer?" Jeffrey whispers to me. "Is that the same as gay?"

"Shh, let her finish."

"We are working on a way for Dani to cross into South Ohio to meet you both. There is a small area of the border that will be rebooted for a short while soon and all security will be off. We are figuring out how to keep it off a little longer. If you have a way to get to a little town in South Ohio called New Hope, include a scene from the parting of the Red Sea in the next papercut. I will let you know exactly when and where soon. Signing off, Pix."

It's not the first time that Jeffrey and I sit in silence utterly astounded by what we've just seen and heard. He finally looks over at me and gives me a playful smile.

"Go ahead, SJ, tell her fairies bring the light and see if she comes back."

I purse my lips and silently tell him I am not amused, which gets him laughing.

As I walk home, I reflect on the fact that there is no such thing as normalcy in my life anymore. Not only do I see souls, I am learning from a woman who sees the future and from a man who is teaching me to defend and attack. I can create and unlock secret codes and comfort my closest male friend who is gay and also one of the righteous thirty-six; and who now seems to have a gay, or should I say queer, pen pal.

What happened to the predictability of sitting at my little desk in the basement after Shabbat, week after week, working on my art? What happened to Judith Braverman who could not figure out what kind of life she should lead other than the one that had been laid out for her?

While it's true that I have no greater clarity now about the course of my life than I did before, I'm beginning to glimpse a faint outline. It's still vague and fuzzy, but I can tell I am destined for something; and it's not the thing I, or my mother, for that matter, would have ever conceived of.

CHAPTER SIXTEEN

Dani

Ibi is hunched over his little fiefdom desk dressed in one of his traditional Igbo outfits. He doesn't wear them every day, but once a month we see him in these bright-colored pullover shirts, wide-legged soft fabric pants and a little wool cap with a small piece pointing up at the top.

I tap his shoulder in greeting and am rewarded with a grunt. "Busy over here, Twenty-Five, in case you didn't notice."

I shake my head. It's not worth starting up with him when he's in this kind of mood. I trust at some point he'll apologize and call himself a derogatory name to make me feel better.

Today he's wearing a rather muted black and white pattern Igbo shirt and his cap is white. On most days, even when he dresses in the casual clothes the rest of us wear, one of the many *taqiyah* he owns sits atop his head. Of the five of us, Ibi is the most religious, smoothing out his prayer rug and getting down on his knees several times a day. We've begun to plan our group meetings around his prayer schedule. Even though Aisha says she has no patience for religion, she does understand the need to be respectful of what she refers to as Ibi's "cultural traditions."

While our country welcomed Muslims after The Split, the tolerance level it shows them, as well as the few religious Catholics and Jews we have, is sometimes shaky. Although it's acceptable for women to wear the hajib head covering, anything that covers more of their face draws instant critiques in our media and newspaper editorials about women's oppression. If a Catholic hospital refuses to perform abortions or won't allow for Death with Dignity decision-making, the health department will begin an inquiry.

For us Jews, the issue is a lot about Israel. While the GFS has full diplomatic relations with Israel, the UPR used to have what it called a "consul relationship" until we launched the boycott, and then Israel cut off diplomatic relations. This, of course, is all about our opposition to the continued occupation and treatment of the Palestinians, a cause I support and have even volunteered for, as have most UPR Jews I know.

But for some people, condemnation of Israel often becomes a slippery slope into condemnation of Jews as a people. My father says this is something we have to pay close attention to, especially as antisemitism tightens its grip in the GFS.

In my little world, it's all about my brother Binyamin, and his decision to become Orthodox and settle in the south. I'm regularly challenged about it and always find myself on the defensive.

"I'm a tyrant and an asshole, Dani, but I'm sure you know that by now." There it is, Ibi's apology.

"Yes, I know," I tell him, and begin to laugh as I head back over to his desk. "What's put you in such a good mood today?"

"Ugh," he responds and slides the paper he's been working on in front of me.

"Ah, analog hard copy?" I say as I lift the paper to read it. "You must really be crazed about something."

"My national service requirement."

I look closely at what he's written. It's a list of the options he's considering with a plus and minus beside each one.

"Hmmm." I begin to read aloud. "Security service. Pluses: can lead to diplomatic position. Minuses: war and weapons." I lower the paper. "Julia and I are doing security service after we graduate. You'd only be a year ahead of us."

"Keep going," he says and waves me on.

"Climate mitigation. Pluses: no weapons. Minuses: intense heat and storms, physical labor." I chuckle. "I agree on the minuses. You know, my mom wants me to sign up for this. Not a big surprise there."

"My mother is all about security," he says. "She thinks one day I'll be made the ambassador to Nigeria."

"Then you could wear the red cap?" I ask.

"Well, I still wouldn't be considered a tribal chief, but they might make an exception for the UPR ambassador. And red is a good color for me."

I shake my head and chuckle. "I'm sure they'll consider that."

"Go on," he urges with another wave of his hand. "There's only one more."

"UPR WPA Project. Pluses: least amount of physical labor involved. Minuses: really hard to get into, especially when you have no artistic talent."

I smile at that last comment and lay the paper down. "You're a decent writer and a great editor, Ibi. That's artistic talent."

"You know how many writers apply? When it comes to getting out of the security service, suddenly everyone's a writer, filmmaker, or artist. It'll be competitive even for Aisha."

"Yeah, but she's determined to get in plus she's got the reparation points."

"Yes, there's that," he says with a hint of disdain in his voice. I know Ibi is a bit conflicted about the fact that Aisha is able to take advantage of the Reparations Act, which not only pays her a yearly allowance but also gives her certain advantages, like getting one of her top choices for national service and a break on a home mortgage. It's not that he's against compensating the ancestors of the former USA slaves, but as an African immigrant himself, he doesn't see how he's any less disadvantaged.

In some ways, I can see his point. Many Black and Brown people were treated horribly and violently by the GFS military during The Split. Those who owned homes or farms were evicted and forced to repatriate to the UPR or be confined to reservations in the boiling hot desert. While the UPR accepted all of them, many were not eligible for reparations payments and affirmative action. Their campaign to be included in reparations has so far been unsuccessful. And with the pressure from climate refugees wanting to live here, I think the government is feeling squeezed and a bit paralyzed.

"I'm surprised WPA isn't your first choice, Dani, what with the photography and the holograms."

"Julia and I have an agreement that we're going to do service together, especially since Trey is signing up for Climate."

"Wow, the couple will be separated for two years. But security service? Why?"

I sit on the edge of his beloved desk challenging him to shoo me off, but he doesn't. I guess this dilemma of his is more important than his usual need for space.

"Promise you won't laugh?"

"No," he responds.

"Well then..."

"Oh c'mon," he says. "I'm even letting you sit on my desk."

I sigh. "Oh okay. I know it's not the most popular thing, especially among the people we both know, but I'm patriotic and I believe the UPR needs to stay safe. Besides, Julia and I think we can get accepted into the intelligence branch and I hear it's filled with queers, so maybe I can get a girlfriend out of the deal."

"So much for patriotism," he says and shakes his head.

"No, it's both."

Kat's high priority notification dings in my head. "Hold on Ibi. My iBrain is dinging. There's a new message from Jeffrey."

Ibi stands. "Great. Let's hear what he has to say. I could use a distraction."

Julia transferred a copy of her decoding program to Kat but I haven't yet used it to read a message from Jeffrey. I call up his email to be projected so Ibi and I can read it together.

Dear Dani,

You asked about my friends. Well, then this will be a very short email. I've always been a kind of loner, mostly of my own choosing. Easier to stay a cynic that way (ha!). But there are a few guys I've been able to relate to on our school's Tech Team, and while I won't say we're super close, I can tolerate them.

Then there's Judith, who I guess I'd now call my best friend. You already know about her artistry. Suffice it to say she also has a good soul (maybe you can do the math for once?). Her best friend Hannah has also become my friend. Hannah is a doer and a woman of courage. I sometimes think she has no fear, which I'm not sure is a good thing. And finally, Isaac, the rabbi's firstborn son and I'd guess you'd call him Hannah's boyfriend. Isaac is what we here would call a mensch. (Picture in your head an old Jewish man with an accent saying, "He's a real person." That old Jewish man is me.) Isaac was nice to me when nobody else was, and to my surprise he has become a good friend, which believe me has elevated my stature here (not that I care of course).

That's the sum total for me. My father says all you ever need is a few good friends, and I guess now I have some.

I'll end by saying that while he's too important and prestigious to count as a friend, your brother has become someone I truly admire. And there are only a few people I'd say that about.

Take care and enjoy this papercut of the Red Sea parting. Judith says to tell you it was a brave Hebrew named Nahshon, trusting in G-d, who took the first step into the sea. I've always thought of Nahshon as a noodnik, but Judith says that the person who takes the first step will always be remembered (as long as he doesn't drown, I'll add).

Jeffrey

"He's funny," says Ibi.

"Yeah." I'm quiet as I again skim the email. "What do you think he meant by me doing the math? There's something he thinks I can figure out about Judith having a good soul."

"Maybe she's also queer?"

"I don't think so. He would have mentioned it when he came out to me." I keep skimming the email. "Why does he leave out the o in God?"

"I don't know much about Judaism," says Ibi, "but from what I know about Islam you wouldn't write the holy name on something that could be erased, so you leave out a letter."

"Strange."

"Only to heathens like you," he says and elbows my arm. His smile tells me he's kidding.

"So is there a hidden message here?" Ibi points to the image of the papercut.

I tell Kat to take a screenshot and enter it into Julia's program, instructing her to read the message aloud so both Ibi and I can hear it. After a few seconds, her voice comes through my device.

"*Judith really can read people's souls.*" I pause Kat and look at Ibi.

"You do the math," he says.

"What does that even mean?" He shrugs. "Maybe there's more to it."

I tell Kat to continue.

"*Meeting is possible. When and where?*" I pause again and smile at Ibi.

"I'm going to meet him!" I say in triumph, pumping my fist high. "Kat, continue."

"*Things getting worse. B Fine lost job at UC. Dept gone. Doing other work now.*"

I sink to my knees. Kat has gone silent. I ask her if there is more and she tells me there is not. My head is in my hands and Ibi has grasped my shoulder.

"Binyamin was fired because the university eliminated the Jewish Studies department."

Julia's voice cuts into my misery. "What is it, Ibi?"

He's videoed all three to be projected into the room. Aisha must see me crying on the floor. "Dani, what is it? Is it Jeffrey?"

Ibi fills them in and there's a chorus of three voices saying, "Be right there."

I am having trouble breathing. "Inhaler," I croak to Ibi.

He rifles through my messenger bag and hands it to me. I'm better after two puffs, but Ibi insists on walking me over to the window for fresh air.

We're both quiet as we wait for the others to arrive. Ibi has a good sense of when it's best to give someone space. All I need from him is to be there in the room with me.

I'm sitting at my usual place, with my head in my hands. What will I tell my parents? My mother will go nuclear when she hears this. She will call the government and start an international incident, all the time railing against my brother and his decision to settle "down there" as she calls the GFS. My father will work his contacts to see if he can sneak Binyamin and his family over the border and risk his own life as well as theirs.

I sit with these frightening possibilities, knowing that regardless I have to tell them. And I hope against hope that they act like rational adults.

CHAPTER SEVENTEEN

Jeffrey

Isaac and I arrive at our usual kiddish table in the back corner of the social hall far from the crowd of people milling around the food. As we take our seats and I nod hello to the girls, Hannah stands.

"I'll get going," she says. "I don't want any trouble."

"Since when?" I ask.

"Jeffrey!" admonishes Judith.

"Hannah," says Isaac in a pleading voice.

Hannah has that look of intensity that unnerves me. "I'll tell you since when," she says, clearly annoyed. "Since the Rebbetzin took one of my campaign flyers for Solly at the bakery Thursday afternoon, handed it right back to me and said 'Feh! I thought you were a nice girl. Stay away from my son.'"

Isaac stares at the table shaking his head. He looks stricken. "Hannah, please stay," he pleads. He sits up and squares his shoulders. "It doesn't matter to me that she feels that way. I'm almost eighteen and soon she'll have no say over what I do or who I'm with."

Hannah looks over at him and her expression softens. She sits on the edge of her chair. I hear Isaac's exhale of relief.

"Besides," he continues, "this will pale in comparison to their reaction when I tell them I'm not going for rabbinical training."

Judith literally gasps and I have no idea if she's appalled at his decision or if she just fears the wrath of the rabbi and his wife. Of the four of us, Judith is the least rebellious, so I never know.

"Then what will you do after high school?" she asks.

Isaac has to pull his gaze away from Hannah to respond to Judith. "I don't know yet. I'd like to go to college, but I'm not sure where."

Most of the UPR colleges have branches in the GFS, but they are subject to GFS academic guidelines. I'm not sure how Isaac would deal with that.

"I was thinking about Hebrew University or Bar Ilan in Israel."

Hannah looks at him in utter shock. "Israel? You'd be away four years?"

"You'd come with me, of course. We'll get married."

Judith and I look at one another and then at Hannah, who in the next few seconds is back on her feet. That scary intense glare reappears, her body rigid, her eyes hard and unblinking.

"Well, Isaac, I'm so glad you've figured everything out for us. All that, without even consulting me. Well done." It's a dose of sarcasm I can normally appreciate except it's directed at my friend.

By the time he calls out "Hannah, wait," she is out of earshot.

Isaac is out of his chair when Judith waves him to sit. "I'll go," she says.

We both sit there for a full minute among plates piled with uneaten food. I have a notion to pilfer some of that wine again because Isaac could probably use it.

He is literally moaning, his forehead flush against the table. "I'm such a jerk, Schwartz. How did I not see this coming?"

"Don't be so hard on yourself, lover boy. She's a strong woman, that Hannah of yours. How 'bout you hold the table and I'll be right back with the schnapps."

As I walk back over to the food table, trying to look as casual as possible, I review the current state of affairs. Professor Fine got the ax from the university, which no longer teaches Jewish Studies. Simeon the snake is marrying the dreaded Yetta. We are all sneaking around working on Solly's campaign, except for me. I don't have to sneak because my father is also working for Solly. I see more horrible spray-painted messages of hate every day. Hannah has walked away from Isaac, who is contemplating a long trip to Israel thus leaving me with twenty-five percent fewer friends. I sigh as I reach for the wine bottle. A fine Shabbes this turned out to be.

The only thing I can look forward to is the meeting with Dani Fine in a few weeks. But even that could go wrong in a million ways. She could get caught. We could get caught. Solly's car could break down. I practically spill the wine all over the table as I contemplate every possible tragic outcome.

Judith has gone back and forth about coming with us to meet Dani. "I'm not as daring as the rest of you. Plus, you wouldn't believe the amount of chores I have now that Shuli is out of the house."

"But Dani is dying to meet you."

"Oh, how do you know that?"

"Because she admires your art. She told me that."

This conversation or some variation of it has occurred many times before I finally enlisted Hannah's help, which of course did the trick.

"I don't want to be the only girl," she told Judith. "How would that look?"

"How does any of this look?" Judith retorted. "So many horrible things could happen."

"And wouldn't you hate yourself if one of them did and you weren't with us?"

I smile remembering that last volley from Hannah, my admiration for her growing every day.

* * *

Isaac very nearly prostrated himself before Hannah and chanted the Great *Aleinu* on his belly, like the rabbis do on Yom Kippur, before she accepted his apology.

I would have thought that Isaac's plan to marry her would make Hannah jump for joy instead of storm off. But as Hashem often told the Hebrews, we are a stiff-necked people, some of us worse than others.

After our latest Krav Maga lesson, Solly is giving Isaac a million detailed instructions about how to operate his Ford hatchback, as if it were a spaceship.

He was originally going to come with us, but with the election and everything, he's worried he'd call too much attention to our little group if the police stopped us. I'm not sure how different it would be when they look up the car and see that it's registered to him, but none of us can get the use of our family's cars for such a long trip and Professor Fine's car would cause just as much attention. So we decide to stick with Solly Herschel.

This New Hope that Dani has decided on is in the middle of nowhere, just south of the border, which runs along I-70 and straight north of Cincinnati. Plus we are all thinking that the name New Hope could be significant. Well, *they* do. I just think it's a name of a one-horse town.

Besides, Dani has it worst of all. She has to hike a few miles over the border and south to New Hope to meet us. Judith and I will only have to walk a short distance once we reach the town to get to the meeting place, which of all things, is a church. Why, Dani? Did you miss the email where I said we were Orthodox Jews?

This news almost made Judith back out of the whole thing, but I was able to persuade her.

"What do you care? They have their religion, we have ours. It's all God in the end."

She grimaced at my logic and shook her head, but at least she agreed to the arrangement.

CHAPTER EIGHTEEN

Judith

The sun has set. Isaac turns on the headlights and Jeffrey plays with the radio dial. Even this close to the border we won't be able to pick up any UPR stations, but we do get a dose of current pop music, something we're normally not able to listen to at home.

Somehow Jeffrey is familiar with this music and every few minutes he's turning around from the front seat to tell me and Hannah how much he likes or dislikes a certain song.

When we first started out on the trip, I suggested we sing something and began with "Hinei Ma Tov." When I next suggested "Am Yisrael Chai," Jeffrey pleaded with me that we "Stop with the Hebrew songs" as he put it, and that's when he began to play with the radio dial.

The trip takes a little over an hour and everything is timed almost to the second because, as Jeffrey explains it, Dani's friend Julia can only keep the border security apparatus for both countries from coming back up for an extra fifteen minutes. Since the actual rebooting also takes fifteen minutes that gives us only a half hour, which has to include the time Dani needs to hike from her car to our meeting place and back. It leaves very little time for us to spend with her, and less if either of us is late.

I may be the only one in the car who isn't enjoying the music. Hannah is swaying in her seat, head nodding to the beat. Isaac is tapping on the steering wheel. I'm getting a little bit of a headache. It might be the music or just the pressure of this entire situation, or both. The car itself is pretty comfortable, the back where I'm sitting with Hannah is roomy and the seat is softer than the worn and creaky material of my father's old van.

"Well, here we are," announces Isaac.

I look up and there's a Welcome to New Hope sign that's barely visible in the dark.

"I'll pull over someplace and the two of you can get out."

"Can't we just all go?" asks Hannah for probably the millionth time.

"Hannah, no," says Jeffrey, exasperated. "Dani is expecting just me and Judith. She's coming alone. We have to follow her plan, otherwise even more things could go wrong."

The thought of having to worry even more makes me intervene to support Jeffrey. I lightly touch Hannah's arm and she turns to me. "He's right," I say in a quiet voice. "Stay here and signal Jeffrey's device if anything should go wrong, just like we agreed."

She nods and the look on her face conveys her grudging acceptance. Then she leans over and hugs me tight. "Stay safe, Judith. I'll see you soon."

I notice Jeffrey and Isaac shaking hands followed by the click of a seat belt unfastening and the opening of the car door.

When I'm outside next to the car, Isaac rolls down his window. "Good luck, Judith. Hannah and I will be right here when you get back. We'll recite psalms." Jeffrey, who is next to me, responds with a little chortle followed by a sarcastic, "Great."

Then we're both walking along the road heading north toward the church, the only landmark of any note in this tiny town. Luckily we don't have to go inside, just meet up with Dani in the parking lot behind the building.

My mother taught all of us never to even go near a church. "They don't want us there and we don't want to be there either," she said.

Like most hard and fast rules I've been taught, I've always accepted this one as the truth. Until now. Until I've started to see how many of the things they are telling us—like there's nothing to worry about when we are being attacked and vandalized regularly—are lies. Or if not lies, then the truth as they'd like us and themselves to believe.

Jeffrey and I are quiet as we walk, unusual for him. He normally expresses his nervousness in a stream of recitations of all the things that could go wrong. But not tonight.

Finally, after less than ten minutes, Jeffrey points to a building in the distance. It's taller than the homes that surround it and has a spire on top. The church.

One light illuminates the small parking lot, which has room for only about a dozen cars, if that. The building is wood and stone; the wood painted a lighter color that I can't make out in the dark.

We look around for Dani. My heart is beating fast and I can hear the faint noise of my rapid breathing.

"There!" he whispers and points to a figure cloaked in the dark who is walking toward us. She appears to be keeping herself away from the beam of light that only covers about half of the lot. Jeffrey follows her lead and steps sideways into the darkness. She's seen us, so we don't need to be all lit up.

She's jogging toward us, smaller than I pictured her. Jeffrey and I look at each other and smile. This is really happening. For the moment I forget all the things that could still go wrong and just concentrate on the fact that we are here and so is she.

When she reaches us, in one movement she pulls off the hood of her black Windbreaker and launches herself at Jeffrey. I can't help but laugh at how shocked he is, his body stiff in contrast to Dani who seems to want to climb on him.

"Jeffrey!" she calls out, louder than any of us should be talking. Then she seems to remember and in a penetrating whisper adds, "You made it!"

He takes a half step back, looking a bit overwhelmed, then a grin appears and he whispers, "Hi."

I'm smiling too, mostly at the thought that Jeffrey is not at all used to girls propelling themselves at him.

In the next instant, Dani and I are facing one another. Her dark hair is wavy and doesn't reach her shoulders, a bit messy from being under the hood. Her face is round and it's too dark to see the color of her eyes. But even with so little light I find something really pleasant about the girl before me, something indescribable.

Before I know it, her soul appears in a multitude of blues—navy, aqua, teal, and the palest color of the sky. As the colors fade, I feel my body being pulled to her. There's nothing I can do but move forward. Something is drawing me closer and it seems to be the same for her. When we meet and touch, it is unlike any hug I've experienced. So different from Hannah's squeeze in the car when she told me to stay safe. So different from my comforting of Jeffrey.

This is more than a hug. It's an embrace. I am in her arms and she is holding me. There's softness and strength and the scent of country air coming off her.

I can't explain what happens next except to say that the same force that pulled me toward her places our lips together and keeps them there. I'm unable to think or even react in the way I would expect. I don't move away. I stay, exploring her mouth, accepting her tongue into mine.

"Dani! Dani, no! What are you doing?"

We break apart at the sound of Jeffrey's angry and distressed voice, both of us breathing hard. The spell, or whatever it was, is broken and I take a step back, staring at the ground, my head shaking.

I can sense Dani moving close to me. "I...I...Judith, I'm so sorry. I don't know what just happened. There was this pull... I'm really sorry."

I don't lift my head and am surprised at the words that come out of my mouth. "Don't be," is all I say. And while I can't believe what I've said, I know it is the truth.

"How much time do we have with you?" Jeffrey asks. A trace of anger remains in his voice.

I look up and Dani is staring at something on her wrist. "Only seven minutes."

She turns to Jeffrey. "Do you want to come with me? You know, in the UPR you'll be able to live openly."

"Did you bring your iBrain?" he asks. Dani and I both look at him. "I've never seen one," he says, as if that explains anything.

She pulls something from behind her ear and gives it to him. We watch as he steps into the lighted part of the lot and begins to study the object in his hand, turning it over and running his fingers along the edges.

Dani and I take advantage of this diversion to gaze at each other. "Come home with me," she whispers. "I don't want to leave you. I know I sound crazy, but..." She trails off.

"You don't," I tell her and there is a moment in which I consider it. That pull, that kiss, my body against hers. What is this and how can I walk away from it?

The image of Dvorah Kuriel comes into my head. She will be able to explain this to me, as she has everything else I'm experiencing. After all, she knew about Jeffrey.

From Jeffrey, I then think about Hannah and Isaac and Solly and Dani's brother, Professor Fine. I cannot leave any of them, even though the pull to Dani is so strong.

Jeffrey hands the iBrain back to Dani. I see a tear roll down his cheek.

"I can't go with you now, Dani," he tells her, his voice choked. "You see, it's because Fredy Hirsch didn't go to Bolivia, and Harvey Milk inspired millions, and Steven Greenberg said you could be Orthodox and gay."

Dani is shaking her head in confusion. Of course she doesn't understand. But I do and I can literally feel my love and admiration for Jeffrey Schwartz expanding in my heart.

"Harvey Milk?" she asks.

"Gay, Jewish heroes," I explain, "all three of them. His spiritual forefathers." And then I add in a whisper, "Maybe even mine."

I go to her for one final embrace. This time I am holding her. "We both have to stay and face this thing, whatever it is," I tell her loudly enough so Jeffrey can hear. "We can't run away from the people who are on our side and need us."

There is one more long, beautiful kiss, and as it ends, I can feel that thing on Dani's wrist vibrate.

"I have thirty seconds and then I have to get back before the border security is turned back on."

I step over next to Jeffrey and she addresses us both. "We will help you, my friends and I. I don't know how yet, but we will find ways."

She reaches back behind her ear and hands her iBrain to Jeffrey. "Here, you can have this. I'm getting a new one. Take it apart and see if you can make it work. In the meantime, Pix will be in touch." She smiles at us. "Good luck."

She's walking backward still facing us. "My brother," she calls out. "How is he?"

"All right," Jeffrey responds. "Teaching at the Yeshiva and working for a great guy named Solly Herschel who's running for office. Your brother's with us."

"I knew he would be," says Dani. "Tell him I love him. And both of you as well. Judith, don't forget me, please. I don't want this to end."

We're both waving to her, and in that last second before she turns to run toward the border, I blow her a kiss. As she blends into the darkness, I am left with the reemergence of the many shades of blue of her magnificent soul. I stand staring at them until the last glittering color dissolves.

"Judith, what just happened?" asks Jeffrey as we head back to the car.

I don't answer for a few seconds, and then in a halting voice, I tell him, "I d-don't really know. And I'm not ready to talk about it."

CHAPTER NINETEEN

Dani

Out of breath from running, I still manage a last burst of speed when I see the lights of the highway up ahead. The border is very close and according to the device Julia programmed for me, I only have seconds to make it through. I sprint across just as the sound of an electronic snap crackles right behind me. I'm through, but I have to keep going so I'm not visible on the monitors.

At last I'm bent over the hood of the AV, trying to catch my breath. Strong arms grab hold of me and the clicking of Aisha's beads are sounds of home. I let her hold me while I recover. But I can't help but notice the difference between this closeness and what I felt with Judith. I'm not even sure I can put it into words. It's like a gift wrapped so beautifully in paper and ribbon bows that you can't bring yourself to open it. So I decide to keep it to myself for a while.

The rest of the group has joined us and crowds around me, talking over one another, asking questions. "How was it?" "Did you meet them?" "Did anyone harass you?" "Did the timing device work?" "What are they like?"

Still panting, I point to the AV indicating that I need to get inside and sit down.

We've gotten a five-seater where we can face one another. Julia has figured out a way to program our destination but shut off all the other tracking systems so there won't be any record of this trip.

I begin with the easiest question first. "The device worked great," I tell Julia. "But I cut it very close and had to really race to get over the border in time."

"We noticed," says Ibi. "I worried it would be hard for you to leave them."

You have no idea, I think and do not reply.

"How are you?" asks Trey, always the one who focuses on feelings.

"Okay, just needing to calm down from this. Glad to be back in the good ol' UPR." I give them a weak smile.

"What's it like over there?"

I'm sure Aisha is asking this because she's expecting that I've seen white hoods and red ball caps everywhere. "It was dark so I couldn't see much. Only regular houses and the church where we met. Nothing outside the norm."

"And them?" asks Ibi. "Did you meet them?"

I nod. "They're great. I gave Jeffrey my old iBrain. They don't have them there."

Julia rolls her eyes. "'Course not."

"He didn't want to come back with you?" asks Aisha. She's been worried about Jeffrey ever since we found out he's gay.

"No, and that surprised me. He went on and on about these guys that Judith called his Jewish gay forefathers. Harvey Milk was one. And there's another one he mentioned, Fredy Hirsch. He said something like 'Fredy Hirsch didn't go to Bolivia.' I have no idea what he was talking about."

"Hold on," says Julia. "I'll ask Che." Julia's iBrain is named for Che Guevara. We all have our heroes.

A male voice speaking Spanish comes out of Julia's iBrain. Since we're all bilingual—it's a UPR requirement—I learn who Fredy Hirsch was, and more important, what he did. An openly gay Jewish man who lived during the Holocaust and took care of children in Auschwitz of all places. Even with all I've read about the Holocaust, I had no idea.

"Wow," says Ibi. "Definitely a hero. I guess he's inspired Jeffrey."

And Judith as well, I muse.

I close my eyes so they'll think I want to rest after my ordeal, but I just want some quiet time to think about her and about what happened.

Her dark curly hair, her soft pliant body, and those kisses. Oh Judith. After only a few minutes, I know that I need to be with you. But I also know that you need to remain where you are for now.

Stay strong and fearless, sweet girl. Gain strength from my thoughts of you and gain courage from your name. Braverman. Be brave.

It's as close as I'll ever come to actually praying. The words in my head are like my private meditation, and I know I'll be returning to them time and again.

CHAPTER TWENTY

Jeffrey

I'm sitting in the back with Judith, hoping to shield her from Hannah's tireless nagging about Dani.

"What is she like?" "Is she pretty?" "Did she say she'd help us?"

I'm the one who answers all these questions, with just a quick yes in response to whether Dani is pretty. Like I would know. Judith is quiet and luckily Hannah doesn't press her.

At the sound of the siren, I turn to see the blue lights approaching. We've been spotted returning from New Hope, only about twenty miles from home.

I bend forward and see Isaac looking into the rearview mirror. He lets out a groan. "Damn," he says and quickly apologizes.

"Isaac, take off your yarmulke," I tell him as I slide mine off my head.

"What? Why?"

"Do you really have to ask?"

"He's right," says Hannah. "Give it to me."

He hands her the black yarmulke he always wears and she pushes it to the bottom of her purse. Judith grabs my hand and squeezes it hard. Isaac is muttering something in Hebrew. I can't tell which prayer it is. How is this guy not becoming a rabbi? He's almost as pious as SJ.

He pulls the car over still muttering and I shush him. Hannah is rifling through the glove compartment and pulls out the car's registration.

Solly and Binyamin Fine had anticipated this scenario. Binyamin said his grandfather told him stories of how police in the former USA regularly pulled over Black drivers, and in some cases, these stops would result in the driver being shot by the police. This happened so frequently that as their children reached adolescence, parents would have what was known as The Talk about what to do if they were stopped by the police. It was basically the same instructions Binyamin and Solly gave us before we set out on this trip. *Stay quiet. Don't offer anything more than you are asked. Be polite and let them always see your hands.*

Our cover story is that we were trying to locate an old friend of Isaac's from summer camp. A boy with the very common name of Joe Kaye. We drove all the way to Eaton, looking for his address, but when we got there we realized we had the number wrong, so we turned around.

It's not the best cover story, but it's not the worst. There's no one we spoke to along the way who they can contact. The address we had was wrong so they can't verify it. And there are hundreds of Joe Kayes. We're just four dumb teenagers who made a mistake.

Isaac opens the window and the figure of a big, beefy cop, like out of an old movie, comes into view. All that's missing are the mirrored sunglasses.

"License and registration," he barks.

I send Isaac a telepathic message. *Don't ask why he pulled us over. Don't ask why he pulled us over.*

He examines the license, holding a small flashlight.

"Lev-en-thal," he says as if he's just learning English. "What kind of name is that? And Isaac. Isn't that from the Old Testament? Is that where it's from?"

"I believe so, sir," Isaac answers in a quiet voice. I can see his hands visible to the officer on the top of the steering wheel. Good. He remembered.

The cop switches his attention to the registration and a puzzled expression comes over his face. "Who's Solomon Hershell? Is that you?" he asks, pointing to me.

Judith releases my hand and I shake my head, too scared to even say the word no.

"Officer," Hannah interjects, and he swivels his big head in her direction. "Here is a signed letter from Mr. Herschel giving us permission to use his car."

I've forgotten that Solly gave this to us, but luckily Hannah hasn't.

He scans the letter. "Okay, all of you out of the car. Hands on the vehicle."

Judith looks at me and I nod.

We're standing in a row next to one another, hands on the car windows along the passenger side.

"Keys," he says to Isaac. This really worries me because I have no idea if he'll give them back. Once he has them, he tosses them up and catches them in his mammoth hand. "I'll hold on to these while I call all of this in. For your sakes, it better check out."

We stand there for what seems like an eternity, but is likely about fifteen minutes, eight hands flat against the windows. Isaac is muttering again. Probably more psalms. Hannah is quiet with her head held high. I'm looking over at Judith, trying to reassure her and anxious that if she bursts into tears I won't know what to say to console her.

At last he returns and stands next to Isaac.

"Mr. Lev-en-thal, what were you and your friends doing on the road tonight?"

Isaac recites the cover story just as Solly told him to.

"And when you couldn't find this Joe Kaye's house, you didn't think to stop and ask somebody?"

This is a trap, but we are prepared.

"No sir. To tell you the truth, I was kind of embarrassed in front of my friends to make such a stupid mistake, so I said we should just turn around and go home."

"And you didn't stop to get something to eat? Like pizza or ice cream?"

"No sir. We weren't familiar with the places in that area, so we just figured we'd get something to eat when we were back in Cincinnati."

I'm once again relieved that Isaac didn't say anything about only eating kosher food.

"Hmmm. I guess you people avoid regular restaurants, don't you?"

"Sometimes, sir."

I worry about that answer but I have no idea what else Isaac should have said.

When he hands Isaac back the keys, I feel my entire body relax, but I don't move from my spot.

"Okay, all of you back in the car, get yourselves home."

At those words we move quickly. I head for the front seat this time, figuring that maybe Hannah will be a better comfort to Judith who looks like she's going to pass out or throw up.

As Isaac puts the key in the ignition, the cop taps on his window and he rolls it down.

"Listen you kids, I don't want to see you out here again. You understand?"

Isaac and I both say "Yes, sir."

"You people stay in your own area with your own kind or next time we won't go so easy on you."

He walks away.

I'm quiet while Isaac begins to pray aloud, audibly praising Hashem. Judith and Hannah join him. Hannah's voice is strong, normal. Judith's falters and I hear her sniff. I turn around to see a tear roll down her cheek. Hannah's arm is around her and I'm almost ready to thank Hashem myself for giving Judith such a friend who knows how to comfort her.

Instead I silently thank Binyamin Fine and Solly Herschel for anticipating what now seems like it was inevitable. And as my friends' voices continue to swirl around me like a protective cloak, I decide it's only fair to join in and thank Hashem for each of them.

CHAPTER TWENTY-ONE

Judith

I'm lucky that my mother is still basking in the bliss of having married off her eldest daughter. I know this is a temporary reprieve from an intense focus on my life, but at least for now she's not monitoring my comings and goings as closely, which is how I was able to go on the trip to meet Dani and spend time working on Solly's campaign. As long as I get my chores done and spend time with Jeffrey, she seems satisfied.

My only worries are about Hannah. Now that Isaac's mother has felt it necessary to tell half the community that Hannah is working for Solly, I hold my breath every time I sit down to a family meal, anticipating that my father will express concern about our friendship. So far that hasn't happened, but in so many ways I feel like I'm living on borrowed time.

All this, and I can't get thoughts of Dani out of my mind. One more thing I have to hide from everyone. Except Jeffrey. I know he's patiently waiting for me to say something. Well, maybe not so patiently. I keep getting these expectant looks from him. Eyes wide, raised eyebrows, head tilted. I ignore them and shake my head that I'm not ready to talk about it.

Yet I'm filled with questions. Before the meeting, I had no sense of what was to come. I was curious to meet Jeffrey's pen pal, this girl from the UPR with her iBrain and hidden holograms. But nothing prepared me for that pull toward her. It came upon me so suddenly, like the appearance of a soul or the *tsaddik* blast from Jeffrey. But this pull wasn't just something I saw and was awed by. It was something I was a part of. The feel of her hands on me. Her lips and tongue. My own fervent kisses.

For days I've sat at my little table in the basement and sketched the scene. Dani lifting the Windbreaker hood off her head. Her smile lighting up the darkness. Our arms wrapped around one another, faces close.

I sketch, wishing it were not so risky to make the papercut, but knowing I cannot. Instead I tear each drawing into tiny pieces and scatter them into various covered trash cans at home and along the route to school.

My first kisses. And with another girl. It makes me wonder, am I like Jeffrey? Do I have the double problem of being both Jewish and gay?

Since learning about his heroes, as he now calls them, Jeffrey would probably bristle at my use of the word "problem." He'd instead say it was an honor, and then he'd likely follow that with some self-deprecating remark, like it's an honor a *schlemiel* like him doesn't deserve.

I smile to myself as I imagine this conversation, and I am so caught up in my thoughts that it takes me a few seconds to realize I'm standing at the front door of Dvorah Kuriel's house hoping she has some explanation for this thing that happened with Dani Fine.

When I tell her, I'm unprepared for the broad smile on her face and the twinkle in her eyes.

"Oh Judith," she says, drawing out the words in wonder, and covering my hand with hers. "It is not every day that we meet our *bashert*. *Baruch Hashem*. *Baruch Hashem!*"

"My *bashert?*"

"Yes," she exults. "The one who is your meant to be. What do the secular people call it?" She thinks for a few seconds and then perks up. "Oh yes, your soul mate."

"But…" I hesitate, still not able to find words.

"Your gift keeps revealing itself to you, Judith. First the regular souls, good and bad, and then Jeffrey and me, and now this. Who knows what else Hashem has in store for you?"

Instead of filling me with expectation, her words frighten me. "I don't mean to sound ungrateful, but all that feels like it's quite enough."

She laughs. "Yes, of course it must. But what I am trying to make you realize is that your meeting Dani was a positive part of your gift, even if it is filling you with questions and concerns. There is a spark of the Divine in this connection you share. That is the nature of a *bashert*. I should know. It is what I felt with my husband, Dov."

At the mention of her murdered husband, I'm filled with sadness. My eyes pool with tears and a sob escapes. "I'm so sorry," I tell her.

Her hand is on my shoulder and she's comforting me when it should be the other way around.

"Do not weep for me Judith. Dov and I had a lifetime of happiness in the years we were together. You know, the psalm reminds us to number our days so that we may live each moment wisely. That is my wish for you and for Jeffrey and your other friends. Don't let a precious moment go by without appreciating what Hashem has given you, especially when it comes to Dani. This is a blessing that may one day mean even more than a great love."

* * *

"Your *bashert*?" Jeffrey says when I tell him. "SJ, wow. If I was spiritually inclined like you and the marvelous Dvorah Kuriel, I'd tell you that yours is the gift that keeps on giving. Instead I'll tell you that there might be something to this whole idea of love at first sight."

I sigh and shake my head at him. "I'm not sure any of it makes a difference since I'll probably never see her again."

"Oh I don't know about that. The Lady Fine seems to be one determined little lesbian."

I shush him when he says that word. It's a term that makes me a bit uncomfortable, to be honest, and I can't help but feel that it doesn't sum up all of who Dani Fine is. As for myself, I'm so far from embracing that word that I can't even say it aloud.

Plus, there are other issues Jeffrey and I need to talk about. Like this little gathering we're on our way to at Rivka Blau's house. I can tell he's nervous about this since Rivka, Binyamin Fine's sister-in-law, is the head of the Jewish Federation of South Ohio. She's the one in charge of the pen pal project.

"What if she gets to know me and thinks she made the wrong decision when she accepted me into the program?" he asks, a hand on his head. He has this nervous habit of adjusting his yarmulke when he's worried.

I remind him that she'd already met him the night we all had Shabbes dinner at Binyamin Fine's house. But still he insists that the more she gets to know him, the worse it will be.

I'm hoping he calms down when she greets the two of us warmly.

The house is on a quiet street in what is the wealthiest section of Adderley Village, our little Jewish enclave. The Blaus live in a house larger than mine or Dvorah's and certainly more lavish than Professor Fine's apartment.

"This is like a mansion," Jeffrey whispers as we're ushered inside by Rivka. I nod, realizing that instead of calming him down, I'm now sharing his nervousness. We walk through a huge living room decorated in white and blue.

"Don't you think they're taking the whole Israeli flag thing a bit too far?" Jeffrey whispers behind his hand. I shush him, afraid he may be fulfilling his own prediction that Rivka will dislike him as she gets to know him better.

There's a large dining room with a table that easily seats twelve. The walls are lined with dark wood and glass china cabinets containing beautifully decorated gold-rimmed dishes and sets of silver candlesticks and menorahs. Because I can't get a close look as we are guided through, I wonder if at some point Rivka will allow me to spend some time gazing at these objects. They are the kinds of Jewish heirlooms that tend to inspire new ideas for papercuts.

At last we reach our destination. A sun-filled room at the back of the house with a glass wall overlooking an enormous backyard with an expanse of perfectly mown lawn and a grove of trees providing the rear boundary.

Professor Fine and his wife Miriam are seated on a small lime-green sofa. Isaac and Hannah each occupy white wicker chairs with green, white, and yellow cushions. Everyone stands to greet us, and as they do, I hear the muted chimes of the front doorbell.

"That'll be our last guest," explains Rivka. "I'll be right back."

There's a silver tea and coffee set assembled on a silver tray on a large white oval table and a platter filled with brownies, cookies, and sliced chocolate babka. Jeffrey doesn't waste a minute filling up one of the little plates stacked next to the platter.

"Ummm babka," he says to Isaac, who laughs. Hannah smiles, rolls her eyes and shakes her head. "What?" Jeffrey asks her.

"Just you," she replies.

Then all eyes are on the doorway where Solly Herschel enters following Rivka into the room.

Once we are all seated, Solly turns to Rivka. "Where's Bernard?" he asks, referring to Rivka's husband.

Rivka lowers her head in what appears to be embarrassment. Her straight honey-blond hair falls forward covering the sides of her face. Then in a flash she is upright, almost regal in her bearing, assuming her role as head of the Jewish Federation of South Ohio.

"Bernard believes we are best served by his absenting himself from this meeting."

The only response is from Jeffrey who closes his eyes and shakes his head, once again calling attention to his negative judgments. I don't react but I can understand Jeffrey's disapproval. Bernard Blau is one of the largest real estate developers in Cincinnati, and not just in our little Jewish area. It's likely that he wants to distance himself from anyone who might be critical of the local government.

"All right, now that we are all here, let's begin this discussion," says Rivka, still seated, her posture perfect. "With the death of the President's daughter and the election to Congress last year of several admitted white Christian supremacists, things are getting worse for our people." She points to Binyamin Fine. "My brother-in-law has been terminated from the university which has closed down its Jewish Studies program." She points to Isaac. "And the violence is escalating. They are now becoming more specific in who they are targeting. It is feeling less and less like random violence by a few antisemitic youths and more like a concerted campaign."

She sips at her cup while all around her our heads are nodding.

"Many of us in the Jewish Federations across the GFS are becoming concerned, and we have added extra security to our offices and to our online systems. But even so, it is getting dangerous to even exchange information knowing that whatever safeguards we put in place can easily be hacked."

I'm surprised when Hannah raises her hand. "Can I add something?"

Rivka nods assent and Hannah launches into the story of how we were stopped by a police officer north of Cincinnati.

"And when he finally let us go, he told us we should stay in our own area with our own kind."

"He actually said 'you people,'" adds Jeffrey.

"Where were you all going when he stopped you?" asks Rivka.

The four of us look at Professor Fine and at Solly who know exactly where we were.

"They were up near the border making contact with my sister."

Rivka's intake of breath is audible. "But how? They could have been imprisoned. And Dani...They would have..." She stops and we can see her shudder.

At the mention of Dani, my mind puts me back in that church parking lot and I once again feel the insistent force pushing me toward her, and then the touch of her lips on mine.

It's only Solly's voice that rouses me. "They were in my car and we had a cover story all worked out. But you're right, Rivka, it was dangerous and they had a close call."

"And Dani?"

"She's okay," says Professor Fine. "But they were all lucky."

"How was this arranged?" asks Rivka. "The government wouldn't allow this kind of email exchange to go through the pen pal program." She fixes her gaze on Jeffrey.

"We created a code," I say in an effort to take the focus off him. But once that sentence is out of my mouth, I worry I've said too much and look over at Professor Fine, biting my lower lip.

"It's okay, Judith. You can tell her," he says.

Rivka sits open-mouthed as I explain about the papercuts and the holograms.

"Our children are brilliant," she says in a loud whisper when I finish.

"So, brilliant children," Professor Fine says and then grins at the four of us. "Put your heads together and figure out a way for all of us to communicate across the GFS with other Jews. We need a method that's faster than the papercuts and one that is completely secure."

I'm disappointed that my papercuts have been dismissed as too slow, because I'm not sure I have anything else to contribute. Hannah's hand on my arm is comforting when she leans over and quietly says, "Don't take it personally."

Jeffrey is on his feet. He actually jumps a bit as he exclaims, "I think I have an idea! But I need to check to see if the person I'm thinking can help us is trustworthy. I'll let you all know."

He takes a few steps toward the doorway, and then turns suddenly. "C'mon SJ," he says, gesturing to me. "And you too, the future Mr. and Mrs. Leventhal. We can't waste any more time sitting around in luxury."

As I get up, I notice Professor Fine and Miriam looking at each other and laughing at Jeffrey's outburst.

As Rivka shows us out, she puts a hand on Jeffrey's shoulder and squeezes it. "Hashem was surely guiding me when I selected you for the pen pal program, Jeffrey."

I see the look of shock on his face and I have to cover my mouth so he won't hear me giggle.

When we're outside on the sidewalk, Isaac says, "So what's your idea, Schwartz, and who is it that you were talking about in there?"

But before Jeffrey can answer, he's interrupted by Hannah who steps toward him until inches separate them. Her face has that I-mean-business look that I usually see when she's on a quest to photograph some new horrible graffiti or broken window. This time I'm pretty sure it's directed at Jeffrey's comment about the future Mr. and Mrs. Leventhal.

She points a finger within a breath of Jeffrey's face.

"You will never, ever refer to me and Isaac that way again, Jeffrey, do you understand?"

Once more I need to stifle a giggle with my hand when I see the panicked look take over Jeffrey, his Adam's apple jumping up and down in his throat.

Isaac apparently feels no such hesitation and is bent over laughing, holding on to his stomach. The sight of him makes me lose all my composure and then there are two of us bent over in hysterics.

CHAPTER TWENTY-TWO

Dani

Trey is seated on the floor of my bedroom leaning against the side of my bed. They are strumming their guitar and singing loud in an effort to drown out the storm that's raging outside. There's one like this—violent with long downpours and constant bursts of thunder and lightning—at least once a month.

When they finish a song we both liked from last summer, they go right into another and this time we're both singing. It's the song that's been called the anthem of Generation One. That's us; the first generation born into the UPR. It's a remake of an old song from my grandparents', or maybe even my great-grandparents' time called "Won't Get Fooled Again." Our version is sung by the Newbies, a nonbinary, mixed race rock band. My dad said the original was sung by a group called The Who. Kind of a cool name. I actually had Kat play me the original.

Trey's version is a slower acoustic take on the song, though we both shout out "We won't get fooled again" as the song ends, only to be followed by Fine House sounding the deafening wah-wah-wah of the tornado alert.

"Quick. Let's get going," I tell Trey.

Trey is holding their guitar by the neck. I grab my iBrain and scoop up Rosa Luxembourg, our calico cat who's been lounging on my bed. How that cat has been sleeping through the storm and the music is beyond me.

"If this is real, there's no place I'd rather be than the Fine underground bunker," shouts Trey over the alarm as we run down the stairs.

Years ago, when we first moved into this house after The Split, my mom retrofitted our basement so we could withstand whatever the changing climate sent our way. She carved out a tunnel under our backyard that led to a secure room far enough away from the house so we wouldn't be buried under any debris if the worst should happen.

My mom has become a national expert on climate mitigation, helping to protect the UPR and other countries from the rising oceans and the storms. That's where she is now; working on the east coast, ensuring that all the wetlands, seawalls, and islands she's designed are saving the parts of New York City and New Jersey that could be saved. Her latest message to my iBrain assured me that all is going well and she will be heading home tomorrow.

Our storm room is pretty comfortably outfitted with plenty of food and 'net access, but of course, no natural light. Fine House shut off its alarm once it detected that everyone has evacuated.

Trey lies down on the brown leather couch with their guitar across their stomach. They are strumming it softly. Trey is big and broad-shouldered with a large belly and arms like tree trunks. But their face, even with the short dark beard, has a softness to it that is also found in their bright green eyes. Julia always says she fell in love with Trey's eyes first.

"How long do you think we'll be here?"

"It's usually about half an hour till Fine House gives us the all clear."

We're quiet for a few minutes. Trey is playing something classical that they learned from their 'net instruction. It calms me after our sprint down here. Lately, when I'm relaxed like this my thoughts turn to Judith and how amazing she felt in my arms. She smelled like the country air that surrounded us. I guess we both did, though I worried she might find me all sweaty and smelly from my hike over the border. But I didn't sense any hesitation from her.

I wonder what she's doing right now and whether Cincinnati is under a tornado warning. My brother says they have them and his synagogue's basement is usually a safe place to ride it out. Does Judith go there too? I hope she has a safe place since the GFS won't acknowledge climate change and would never let my mom offer any help.

"You're a quiet one, Twenty-Five." Trey smiles at the use of Ibi's nickname for me. I decide to ignore it. Thinking about Judith always puts me in a good mood and places everything else into perspective.

I'm sitting on the carpeted floor next to the couch with my arms wrapped around my knees. "I was thinking about something," I tell Trey. "Actually someone."

They stop picking at their guitar strings and sit up. "Oh? A new crush, maybe?"

"More than that. Look, I haven't told anyone about this because it's incredibly strange as much as it's incredibly wonderful."

"Well now, you gotta spill. I'm way too curious. Oh, and before you make me raise my hand in an oath, I promise not to tell anyone. Except Julia that is. No secrets between us."

"Yeah, that's fair." I sigh, wondering how to begin. I join Trey on the couch so we're level with one another. "The night I went to meet Jeffrey, Judith was with him."

"Yeah. Wait. You mean, it's her you're talking about? The religious girl?"

I put my hand on their knee. "Please Trey, don't interrupt me. Let me just get it all out."

And I do, the whole story, including the invisible force that pushed us together, the softness and the kissing that felt like nothing else would ever be as right as that.

At some point while I'm talking, Trey's mouth opens in shock and remains that way until I stop. Then they punctuate the end of my story with one word. "Wow."

In the silence that follows, Fine House gives us the all clear. But we don't move from the couch in the safe room. It feels like the right place to be talking about this.

"Do you think you'll ever see her again? I mean, you can't go sneaking over the border on a regular basis."

I pull my feet up onto the couch and am once again sitting with my arms wrapped around my legs. I stare at my knees. "I don't know. I just can't stop thinking about what happened, and about her."

"You know, I get all the woo-woo stuff, but Dani, you don't even know this girl."

"Yeah, but I'm having a hard time convincing myself that even matters."

I stand, signaling to Trey that we can go back into the house. The danger has passed for now, and there's nothing more to say about Judith Braverman.

CHAPTER TWENTY-THREE

Jeffrey

The Tech Team room at Kushner Academy for Boys is small. There's a desk with an aging PC and an old laser printer on top. The metal shelves along one wall hold old tablets and laptops, and a selection of peripherals like projectors and scanners. At one time or another, I have had to fix or retool just about everything here, scavenging my father's supply room for parts and using the 3-D printer more times than I can remember.

I'm sitting wedged into a space between Meyer Lipsky in his wheelchair and the wall. Meyer's book bag is hooked onto the back of his chair and there's a white piece of paper peeking up at the top. I glance over as unobtrusively as possible, though really it's unnecessary since Meyer is glued to his computer screen and from experience I know nothing will distract him.

What I see delights me. Meyer Lipsky is walking around, I mean rolling around, with a Solly Herschel for City Council flyer in his bag.

"Lipsky, are you supporting Solly Herschel in the election?" I ask, just to make sure.

He breathes out a sigh, annoyed for being interrupted. "What if I am, Schwartz?"

I place my hand on his shoulder, and then remember how dangerous it could be for me to touch another boy and retract it quickly. "Well then I'd say we have much to discuss, my man."

This is the big break I've been hoping for. Meyer Lipsky knows hardware like no one else, much more so than me or even my father. He's the sultan of circuits, the emperor of electronics, the maven of multicore processors. I could go on all day.

Meyer has not taken his eyes off the screen. His fingers are flying over the keyboard even as he keeps talking. "What's there to discuss? You heard that professor who lectured us a while back. It's like Germany in the nineteen-thirties here. And you know who the first ones were to get eliminated? I'll give you a clue. They were called a drain on society because they were a bit slow, or they couldn't hear or see, or…" He pauses for effect. "They weren't able to move using their legs. Get the picture?"

I nod. What can I say to that?

"It's not like I'm optimistic about Solly's chances," he continues. "But there's so little else I can do to try to make a difference."

"There is something, Lipsky." I reach into my pocket and feel the hard plastic of the device resting there. "Have you ever seen an actual iBrain?"

He lets out a short laugh. "Right, like we can go into a store and buy one. Maybe if I wheel around outside, I'll find one lying on the ground."

"You won't need to. I have one right here."

I finally say something that tears him away from the screen and the keyboard. "Holy shit, Schwartz," he exclaims as he looks at the device sitting in my open palm. "Where did you get that?"

I watch as he looks around our little office, worried that there might be hidden cameras.

"We're okay here, Lipsky."

"One can never be too sure. Let's get out of here and you can fill me in. But I doubt we can make this thing work in the GFS."

"That's where you come in, my friend. You want a way to make a difference? Well, between your genius and my dad's 3-D printer, we are going to manufacture an entire army of iBrains. And very soon I'll be able to get the information we need so we can get this thing to securely link into the 'net."

* * *

"So Lipsky the Magnificent actually drafted a blueprint for the construction of more iBrains, circuits and all," I tell Isaac, Hannah, and Judith during the Shabbes kiddish. "It seems Lipsky's father worked on the original prototype for what became the iBrain before he and his family emigrated to the GFS. So Meyer was able to figure out how to connect the device to human brain waves." I shovel a forkful of food into my mouth and continue. "I've started to print out the parts on the 3-D."

Hannah holds a hand in front of her eyes and looks away. "Jeffrey, please, not with your mouth full."

I gulp the food down quickly. "Sorry, kugel and iBrains, hard to choose which comes first."

"You do have a point," says Isaac, who earns a reproachful glance from Hannah followed by a tiny giggle from Judith.

"Attention, attention, please!"

The entire social hall is interrupted by the booming voice of Barak Rausch, father of the snake Simeon, annoyingly cutting into our peaceful Sabbath. He's at the front of the room, tall, broad and imposing. A frightening reminder of his horrible son.

Holding up a plastic cup of wine in a raised hand, he bellows, "I want to offer a blessing to the Holy One, Blessed Be He, for the great fortune He has bestowed upon my family. As many of you already know, my eldest son Simeon will marry the lovely Yetta Freundlich."

It should be a sin for anyone to place the words "lovely" and "Yetta Freundlich" in the same sentence. The meaningful look Judith and Hannah give one another confirms my suspicion they would agree.

"And now I want to share some more *naches* with all of you. Upon his graduation from our esteemed Kushner Academy for Boys, Simeon will be entering the city's police academy, with a spot reserved for him in our own local precinct."

Oy, now my abuser will have a gun and the force of the law behind him to do more forcing of me and who knows who else. There's some murmuring in response to this news and a few actual "mazel tovs" can be heard above them.

"So, let me offer our blessing of gratitude, but before I do, I want to remind you all to vote in the upcoming city council election." He's smiling now so that we won't have any trouble understanding the meaning behind his words. "And, of course, I hope you will vote the right way."

And off he goes with the Hebrew blessing over the wine, followed by the prayer for gratitude, and if that isn't enough, his hour upon the stage ends with the *Shehecheyanu*, expressing the mistaken belief that we should thank God for letting us share in this momentous occasion. As soon as all the praying is finished, Barak points to his son and motions for him to stand. And what do these poor schnooks in our congregation do? They applaud. There's more "mazel tovs," and during this finale I excuse myself to hit the restroom so I don't upchuck the kugel all over my friends' laps.

If this family was not scary enough, I now have to worry not only that Simeon will be given a badge and a gun, but his father will beat Solly Herschel and become our local elected official.

I sit in the last stall willing myself to keep my lunch in my stomach and unlatch the door when I'm sure I'll be okay. Feeling a bit calmer, I decide to splash some cold water on my face and go back.

But whenever is my life that simple?

When I open the stall door who should be standing there but Simeon Rausch with a big smile aimed at me.

"Schwartz, don't you think a little personal congratulations are in order?"

He grabs hold of my arms, pinning them against my body, shoves me back into the stall and pushes me downward so he can force me onto my knees.

As always, I don't say a word, but I don't have to because thanks to Solly's training my actions are about to ricochet around this bathroom like a siren. I body-slam him so hard he's flung out of the stall. I try to make a run for it, but he rushes at me and I pivot to the side to avoid him. Then I thrust his head back by pushing up against his septum, which makes him lose his balance and fall onto the floor with a loud groan when his head hits the tiles.

I walk backward toward the bathroom door making sure he hasn't gotten up, but to my great relief all he's doing is looking up at me in shocked surprise. That's when I all but bump into Isaac standing just inside the door.

"Someone has learned a thing or two," he says and grins. "I'm sure he deserved to get thrown down, but what happened between the two of you? Did he try to hurt you?"

Only Judith knows what Simeon has been doing to me, and the thought of telling Isaac fills me with shame. He's so good, so perfect and pious, that I can't imagine what it would do to our friendship if he found out.

I settle on something that is a version of the truth. "He insulted me and started pushing me around. It wasn't the first time but I think it might be the last."

Isaac nods in agreement. "Just be careful once he has that badge, so you don't get arrested for assaulting an officer."

I sigh in resignation. "Yeah, I know."

CHAPTER TWENTY-FOUR

Judith

I watch in awe as Jeffrey prints out little black plastic pieces that will soon be fitted together to create an iBrain. An array of small wires and other bits of metal, already printed, are laid out on the table. He's explained that Meyer Lipsky, who Jeffrey refers to as Einstein The Second, is duplicating something called the central core chip for the device. This core chip, Jeffrey says is "worlds beyond" the technology we have in the GFS. It's a relief that someone that smart is working with us and not against us.

Meyer Lipsky is holding one of these tiny pieces of wire as he stares down at what looks like a chart with shapes and lines connecting them. As always, I start thinking about what kind of papercut it might make.

"Is your friend Hannah still going with the rabbi's son?"

It takes me a few seconds to understand what Meyer has asked me. His eyes are still focused on the paper laid out in front of him.

"Lipsky has a thing for your pal, Hannah," Jeffrey interjects before I can answer. "And yes, she's still got Leventhal in her sights, though sometimes she has a funny way of showing it."

I have no idea what Jeffrey means by that last statement. Hannah talks about Isaac all the time when she and I are walking home from school. She's either telling me about the last time they were together or is trying to figure out when she can see him again, especially given his mother's efforts to keep them apart. I turn to Jeffrey and squint, wordlessly asking him to explain.

"You remember, SJ, when she got on my case about calling her the future Mrs. Leventhal and then when she got angry at Isaac because he assumed they'd get married and move to Israel? I mean, if she really wants to be with him, why get all huffy every time the subject of marriage comes up? Maybe Lipsky has a shot at her after all?"

I decide to ignore his comment about Meyer because the idea of Hannah thinking about any boy other than Isaac is just ridiculous. I shake my head and give Jeffrey a pointed look, silently scolding him for getting Meyer's hopes up. "You don't know her the way I do. She's very independent and doesn't like people making decisions for her. That's why she reacted the way she did. But she still has her mind set on Isaac and I'm pretty sure he feels the same way about her."

Meyer is staring at the printer as the whirring of the machine stops and the next piece of molded black plastic sits completed on the base of the machine. "This is the last one we need," he says in a quiet voice.

I feel badly for disappointing him, but it's probably best he knows for certain that Hannah is off limits. Maybe then he can turn his attention to some other girl. As long as that girl isn't me.

While Meyer works with the metal pieces and Jeffrey fits the plastic ones together, I look around for something to do to occupy myself. I'm hoping they finish soon so Jeffrey can read the latest email from Dani. He's been waiting until they've printed the first iBrain because we know there's something hidden in the email that will tell us how to get the device online. But even though that will be the focus of Dani's message, the thought of hearing anything from her both excites and unnerves me. Nothing has changed since that night in the church parking lot. I can still feel the warmth of her embrace and the sweetness of our urgent kisses. And I'm still at a loss to explain any of it.

I busy myself with paper, a pencil, and a small scissors I find in a wooden cabinet in the far corner of this tiny room behind Mr. Schwartz's shop. I'm drawing freehand but realize after a few strokes that I'm actually duplicating the circuit diagram for the iBrain. I quickly fit the lines together so they look like a menorah and not the inner workings of a forbidden device.

"Okay, open the email, Schwartz," Meyer says, his voice eager and a bit too bossy for my taste. "Let's see if your friend in the north can get this thing to work."

I set aside my Chanukah papercut, which I'd like to send to Dani eventually. It seems lately everything I do ends up as a gift for her.

The email appears on the screen. I read it slowly, swatting away Jeffrey's hand when he tries to scroll down to get to the end. He sighs, but then sits back and lets me savor her words.

"C'mon Judith," Meyer whines, clearly annoyed.

"Give her a minute," Jeffery tells him.

Dani is talking mostly about school, or whatever it is she calls it. Then there's a whole part about her friend Trey who plays the guitar and writes songs. It's strange how when she refers to Trey, instead of saying he or she, she says them. It's kind of confusing like she's talking about more than one person. I want Jeffrey to ask her about that.

She ends the email with a story about a recent storm and how their house warns them when a tornado is nearby.

I look up at Jeffrey and tilt my head to the side. "I don't get why she calls Trey they or the part about the house and the tornado."

Meyer groans and speaks quickly. "I have no idea why she talks about her friend that way. But I do know that people in the UPR have smart technology in their homes that controls everything you can imagine, including warning them when they need to go somewhere safe. It's a more advanced version of the Helpers we have."

"My dad hates the Helpers," Jeffrey says. "He says they're linked into the government."

I'm not sure whether I should believe this. "We have Helpers all over the house. We use them for recipes and for turning the lights on and off."

"Well then SJ, I'd suggest you don't have any sensitive conversations when you're at home."

Meyer grips the arms of his wheelchair and throws his head back. His voice sounds like he's being strangled. "Can we please get on with it?"

Jeffrey gets the Weissberg Torah on the screen. Dani's email referenced a verse from the story of Noah. I guess since she was already talking about a big storm, it seems fitting. But I'm worried, since my original code hidden in the papercut also pointed to a section of the same part of the Torah. I don't want us to include something in these emails that would make anyone suspicious. I wish I could tell her to be more careful in the future, but all I can do is send that silent thought out to her and hope somehow that Hashem helps her get it.

The numbers Dani included in her email, 1-9-7-1, refers to the year that a song Trey sang was popular, give us what we need to decipher the code. While I'm working it out, I hear Meyer's impatient groans and audible sighs.

"Lipsky, calm down," says Jeffrey. "She has to make sure she gets this right."

"Just explain this to me later and I'll write a sequence that'll give us the message in less than a second."

And there it is again. That feeling that I'm no longer useful. That my abilities are slow and old-fashioned. I stare at the words of Torah on the screen, now a bit out of focus as my eyes water as I realize that this is likely the last time I will be asked to work out Dani's coded messages.

I push myself to finish and my voice shakes as I read, "Hit reply and type o-w-l."

The message makes me smile when I remember that Owl is the nickname that Dani's friend Ibi assigned to Julia, the girl who was able to keep the border open for an extra fifteen minutes so that Dani and I could...

The light from the screen signaling the appearance of Pix interrupts my thoughts. She's still in that short dress holding the same wand as last time.

"Hi Jeffrey, today I have a message from Owl, but first I'm going to wait for you to get a recording device before I give it to you because it's long and detailed. When you're ready, enter the same three letters again."

She stands quietly, waving her wand with a flourish and releasing pink and purple stars that float around her and then fade away. They remind me a bit of how I see souls.

Meyer holds his device up to the screen. His eyes are wide and all traces of his impatience are gone. He's actually smiling. "Okay, I'm recording this. I don't know if she'll come out on the video, but we should be able to get the audio."

"I'll write down as much as I can in case something goes wrong," I tell them, hoping I can once again be of some help.

Jeffrey types the three letters and Pix comes back to life. Her message sounds like a bunch of random letters and numbers with symbols like parentheses, dashes, and asterisks thrown in. None of it makes sense to me, but I assume it does to Meyer and Jeffrey who are both slack-jawed in amazement. I write as fast I can, hoping I'm getting most of it. Then I'm relieved when Pix's message returns to a language I understand.

"This will give you an hour a day of connectivity. We're working on getting you more, but that might take a while since we want to make sure this is secure. Your hour is six a.m. to seven a.m. Sorry so early, but it's safest."

Meyer bends forward and slides the paper I'd used toward him. I swivel my head, trying to get a fix on his soul, and there's a very brief silver flourish of shiny confetti that disappears into the air. It's good enough and certainly not evil. But even so I'm eager to tell Hannah how annoying he is, even though I'll probably be committing the sin of *lashon hara*, or gossip, which I'll then have to repent on Yom Kippur after I apologize to Meyer. But I can't worry about all that now. I'm more focused on his infuriating behavior.

I do notice that Meyer hasn't played the recording he made and is instead relying on my written transcript. I'm about to say something when Pix begins to speak again.

"Okay, now I have a private message from Dani to Judith. I'll wait until Judith is alone in the room. Please type the letters when you are ready."

"C'mon Lipsky, out we go," says Jeffrey.

"Wait, Schwartz. Why do we have to leave?"

"You heard the pixie, it's a private message. Do I need to create a secret code for you to understand the meaning? Private. Message. Now out."

Jeffrey once again endears himself to me and makes me wish I could love him and he could love me in a way that would make us both fit in. But instead he and I have something else—something no less significant or profound than romantic love. Once again I tear up but this time I'm not filled with self-doubt but instead with affection.

When the door closes behind me, I enter o-w-l and Pix comes to life.

"Judith, this is from Dani. Hi. I hope it's okay to send you this message. I hope you don't hate me. Please don't hate me. Because I can't stop thinking about you and about that night. I don't understand it, but I know it was real. Not just what happened, but what I was feeling. What I'm still feeling. Judith, I've never prayed in my life, but now every night I pray that you are safe, that you can be brave like your name, that you can feel good about what happened and about me. I don't want you to hate me. I want the opposite. Please take care of yourself, sweet girl. I will do everything I can to be with you again. That is, if you want it."

And with those last words, Pix disappears from in front of the screen, fading into the same purple and pink stars and then to nothing.

A tear rolls off my chin onto the projected keyboard landing on the letter X.

CHAPTER TWENTY-FIVE

Dani

My mother can be so annoying. There's no reason for me to be on lockdown today. Just because the Anarchists are in the streets demonstrating again, she thinks it's unsafe to go out. The education district closed all classes and project rooms so I can't even bargain with my mother to let me go to what constitutes school for me. I just get to sit here worrying that Judith hates the Pix hologram I sent her, and by extension, hates me.

The Anarchists are out there because a bunch of the unions are striking. The video I watched this morning was unreal. One faction of Anarchists, the Sacco and Vanzetti Cell, opposes the unions on principle, viewing them as antiquated hierarchical structures. The Emma Goldman Cell, on the other hand, supports the rights of workers to self-organize through unions. Both believe in violence as a way to bring about change, which is why I'm sitting in my house plagued by an endless loop of insecurity, anxiety, and boredom. The only thing that's bringing me a bit of peace is the thought that Jeffrey now has the code that will enable him to use the iBrain for an hour a day.

"Aisha Wright-Bukari is at the front door." This announcement by Fine House and my response to let her in means that I can finally focus on something other than my obsessive self-absorption. I hear footsteps on the stairs and then a few seconds later Aisha appears in my room.

"Ready for me to bust you out of this joint?" she asks and grins at me.

It's still easy to get taken in by those shining dark eyes and high cheekbones, plus the mass of long, thin braids. She's definitely a looker. But since that night with Judith, my attraction to Aisha has transformed from one filled with aching regret over our breakup to an aesthetic appreciation of my very gorgeous friend.

"You know my mother has made this place escape proof."

She sits down on my bed and takes a very large bag of M&Ms out of her backpack. "I know and I'm sure that's against all of the tech laws."

"Not when parents do it."

"Well, as a consolation, I've brought you your drug of choice." She dangles the bag and swings it in an arc, like a pendulum.

"You know me well," I say and take the bag out of her hand, rip open the top and pour a bunch into her open palm. "You were down at the demos today, right?"

"You know *me* well," she says and tosses the M&Ms into her mouth. "It got a little crazy with smoke bombs and tear gas. I went to support the Emmas, but those S&V white boys and their brand of violence aren't my thing."

"Same here. Even if I could have gone, I'm not sure I would have."

"Soooo," she says before reaching back into the bag and sliding a blue M&M into her mouth, "I actually didn't come over to break you out of prison."

"Good thing since it would have been kind of futile." I throw a small handful of the candy into my mouth.

"You'll laugh, but I need to talk to your mom."

I swallow with loud gulp and my chest rises in a chuckle. "Are you in a fighting mood? She's very good at that. Take it from one who knows."

Aisha leans toward me on the bed. "No, it's my Gullah-Geechee project. I need to talk to her about the climate mitigation stuff."

When she's not demonstrating with the Emmas or hooking up with some girl, Aisha has been hyper-focused on helping the small communities of people of color still living in the GFS. This started out as a school project but has taken on a much larger role in her life. All year she's been researching anything she can find on the reservations scattered about the GFS–Vietnamese in Texas, Black Evangelicals in West Texas desert, Native people in South Dakota and the Gullah-Geechee Nation, who live along the southeast coast and are struggling to hold on to their islands as the ocean rises. This community of Black folks descended from slaves are of particular interest to Aisha since she can trace her lineage back to them.

I swallow another mouthful of M&Ms and point to the iBrain that is fastened just above Aisha's ear. "Just read my mom's PhD thesis. It'll save you the aggravation of having to talk to her."

Aisha shakes her head at me. "You know, your mom's not that bad."

I shake my head at her in response. "Then why am I a prisoner in my own house?"

"It's her twisted way of caring?" she offers.

"No, just twisted. Anyway, I'm not sure she has any updated intel on the Gullah-Geechee. The GFS is a bit stingy when it comes to letting anyone find out how their BIPOC are doing, if they're all still alive that is." I sigh and flop down on my back. The mattress bounces a bit from the impact. "I wish your people had accepted the UPR's offer to move to the islands in the Pacific Northwest."

"My people wouldn't be a people without their land. You know that. Besides, I have an idea about how to contact them."

"My mom's been trying for years, working with universities and UPR government people. There's no way."

She's grinning; an index finger pointed at my face. "Oh, but you're forgetting. Thanks to you and the Owl, there are now iBrains in the GFS and maybe Jeffrey or your brother can figure out a way to get one to the South Carolina coast."

I sit up and pop a few more M&Ms in my mouth, sucking off the hard shell to get to the soft chocolate underneath. I'm mulling over Aisha's idea, which isn't half bad except for the assumption that it would be easy for Binyamin to just go on a vacation to the coastal islands without drawing anyone's attention. Plus, if he got stopped and the iBrain was discovered, well, I don't want to even think about what might happen.

The velvet texture of milk chocolate in my mouth is a comfort and takes me away from my thoughts of doom and disaster. Aisha hits me on the thigh and says, "Well?"

I pull my leg back. "Stop with the hitting. You don't want people to think you've taken up with the S&V boys."

"Like I care what anyone thinks." She says this with that haughty tone and a quick uplift of her head. And she wonders why we call her the Gullah Princess. "My idea about the iBrain is pretty amazing, right?"

It's far from amazing, but it is something that hasn't been tried. So it's worth a shot. "Yeah, it could work, but there are a lot of ifs."

"If the Gullah had a way to contact Jeffrey, then we could get information through the papercut code. You see—" She's interrupted by a loud pinging sound that ricochets off the walls of my room.

Aisha has her hands over her ears. "What the fuck, Dani? Is that your tornado warning?"

"Kat, turn off notification," I say in a loud voice so I'm heard over the pinging. "It's a special notification I set up when I get an email from Jeffrey."

"That's insane. A person could go deaf from that."

What I don't tell her is that the real reason I set this up was so I'd know the minute anything came that could include a message from Judith.

I call up a projection of the email so we can both see it. I know there won't be anything I might not want Aisha to see since the text of the email could be screened by the GFS. We silently read about how much Jeffrey hates school, a regular topic, and about all the foods he's eaten in the past week, also something he talks about a lot. Aisha rolls her eyes, sighs and shakes her head. "The boy loves his kugel, I guess." She pronounces it with a hard u.

"It's koogel," I tell her. The u is soft.

"Whichever, let's see the papercut so we can find out what he really wants to tell us."

Even though I know the important stuff is hidden in the code, I still enjoy Jeffrey's emails. His detailed descriptions of food are hysterical. In this email he talks about what he calls the creamy kugel, but in one of the emails he sent last month he included an entire treatise on all the different kugels he's eaten, and the pros and cons of each. Who knew there were five kinds of noodle kugel? The only one my mother brings home from the deli on special occasions is the kind with the golden raisins.

"Wow," says Aisha when I enlarge the photo of the papercut. "It's gorgeous."

Just like the artist who made it, I think. Of course, Aisha's right. The Chanukah scene with a menorah and nine burning candles and a group of four children sitting on the floor playing dreidel, plus a table filled with a stack of latkes, is so lifelike, I feel like I could just walk into that scene and fill my plate with food. In addition to the white paper meticulously cut, almost sculpted to reveal the picture, Judith used an orange background to bring the flames of the candles to life, blue for the dreidel game, and brown for the latkes.

I stand in front of the picture in awe of the talent that could create such perfection, wishing I'd taken a picture of her that night in the church parking lot.

"Dani, snap out of your trance unless you want me to hit you again."

"You have no appreciation for great art," I say as I screen shoot the papercut so it can be read into the decoding program.

In an instant the message comes up on the screen: "THE OWL IS HOOTING AN HOUR A DAY. PRINTING MORE. JB SAYS I WANT THE OPPOSITE TOO."

Judith wants the opposite too. What does that mean? The opposite of what?

I see Aisha's arm raised pointing to the message on the wall screen. "So the owl is Julia, of course, and that must mean they've got the iBrain working for an hour a day, just like she set it up, right?"

I'm still wondering about the opposite of what, wracking my brain trying to figure out what she means.

This time Aisha puts a hand on my shoulder and shakes it gently. "Dani? Dani! Where the hell did you go?"

"Uh, sorry. Yeah, the iBrain seems to be working," I tell her, but even I can hear that my voice has a faraway quality to it.

"And he's making more of them?"

I back up a few feet and sit on the side of my bed. "Yeah," I say, still distracted. She wants the opposite too. Too? Meaning like me? I want the opposite?

And then it comes to me like a flash of lightning, and I quickly stand up. It was the message in the hologram. I said I want the opposite of something. That's what she's talking about.

But before I can call up Pix, there is a hand on each of my arms holding me in place. Aisha is bent down in front of me.

"Dani, you need to tell me what's going on." There's worry in her voice instead of impatience. I must be scaring her.

I sit down again with the realization that this confession was bound to come out sooner or later. Might as well get it over with.

"Well, you see…" And I tell her about that night and the magnetic force and the kissing.

"Oh my God," says Aisha. "She must have freaked out."

"That's just it. When Jeffrey stopped us and I realized what happened, I told her I was sorry and…" I trail off remembering what sounded too good to be true even now. I lower my head and shake it, still floored by her response. I realize I'm smiling.

"What? She said *what?*"

I speak slowly, savoring the memory. "When I told her I was sorry, she said don't be."

Aisha tucks a finger under my chin and lifts my head. She has a big toothy grin on her face. "Good Dani, that's really good."

"I know, but I worry that now that she's had some time to think about it, maybe she's changed her mind."

"And maybe she hasn't. What did that part of the message mean by 'JB wants the opposite too?'"

"I think I know, but I need to do something to make sure."

I call up the last hologram from Pix and fast-forward through all the code Julia sent Jeffrey until I get to the private message I sent Judith.

"This part is a bit sappy. No judge-arino, okay?"

She holds a hand up. "No judge-arino," and she smiles at me.

And there it is in my message. "I don't want you to hate me. I want the opposite."

When Pix fades out, Aisha and I stand together in silence until I hear her whisper, "She loves you."

"I don't know but I hope so."

CHAPTER TWENTY-SIX

Jeffrey

My father is busying himself with the refreshments so he won't have to talk to anybody. I walk over to help him so I won't have to talk to anyone either. Like father, like son. Both pathetic. I stuff my mouth with potato chips while I set out the cookies and pastries, eying the chocolate rugalach for later.

Solly's election headquarters, a small storefront with a second room where we have our Krav Maga lessons, is filling up with people. Hannah is across the room, smiling and trying to be nice to Meyer Lipsky though I'm sure Judith didn't hesitate to share her version of how he behaved the day we printed out the iBrains and read Dani's email.

Yeah, he's not the most warm and fuzzy guy, that Lipsky, but on the other hand, it's only because of him that we have functioning iBrains in the GFS. I figure when you balance his flareups of irritability and rudeness, laced with an annoying dash of Mister-Know-It-All-ness, against his incredible genius, the scale tips toward the Einstein side. In the end, the equation points to the fact that it's worth putting up with him.

One of Solly's campaign people has been keeping a tally of the precinct votes on a whiteboard. The room erupts in applause when he enters the latest numbers showing Solly winning my neighborhood. It is sweet seeing my father raise his fist in triumph. He'd been going door-to-door, debating and arguing with the neighbors, and I guess winning over some of them.

But this is the first precinct total in Solly's favor. The first three up on the board went to the awful Barak Rausch and, by extension, his despicable son.

While I'm contemplating whether to take out my device and do some calculations to determine if Solly still has a chance, I hear a woman calling my name. It's Rivka Blau, looking her usual all-business self in a dark gray skirt and matching jacket, her blond hair pulled up on top of her head.

She waves me over and I follow her into the second room, hoping she is not going to ask me to show her how I used Krav Maga to flip Simeon Rausch onto his back in the synagogue men's room. I quickly wipe my mouth to remove all traces of potato chip crumbs and grease. After all, this is the woman who has the power to cut me off from Dani with the click of a mouse.

I wish Judith was here to reassure me, but she wasn't able to avoid attending the Rausch campaign party with her parents, especially since her father's stupid newspaper endorsed the guy. Isaac was also forbidden from going anywhere near Solly's place, and ever since his mother went on the warpath against Hannah, they're watching him like a hawk.

Rivka is wearing some kind of strong perfume that rich ladies wear, lavender or vanilla or floral or all three, I'm no expert on this stuff. I'm just hoping it doesn't make me sneeze in her face.

She leads me into the second room, but doesn't close the door since it wouldn't be proper for us to be alone. Boxes are piled up against the far wall, probably leftover campaign literature, and some tables and chairs that were moved from the front room for the party.

I remind myself that Rivka Blau and I are on the same side. I have had to keep telling myself this over the past week as we printed out six iBrains for her and some of the other Jewish

Federation people. Lipsky thought I was insane to do this, but Judith convinced me Rivka could be trusted. After all, she is kind of related to Dani.

After an exchange of "how are you" pleasantries and a little commiseration about Solly's likely defeat, Rivka gets down to business.

"I just came back from the nation's capital in Dallas for the GFS Jewish Federation's annual conference. There are five people who now each have a, um," she pauses and then whispers, "device. Please know that these are people I would trust with my life. They are all very clear about the threats we face and want to keep connected to one another in a way that'll be secure. We even decided to give our little group a name. We're the IJN, the Independent Jewish Network."

She smiles, likely supposing I'll think this is a bit hokey, like a bad spy movie. Then she opens her black leather purse and takes out a small paper. "Here are their names and locations. Please keep this information in a safe place."

I nod, slip the paper into my pocket still clutched in my hand.

She is all serious again. "Jeffrey, what you are doing is incredibly important to our people. You may even be helping guarantee that we have a future."

She looks at me with a half-smile on her face, lips tightly together. I want to squirm and step back under her gaze, but I force myself to stand still.

When she finally speaks, her voice is filled with emotion, almost shaking. She briefly lays a hand on my shoulder. "You deserve a good future, God willing, with a loving wife and beautiful children."

The half-smile is back for a few seconds as if she's letting her little prayer sink in. Then she takes a step toward the door and waves me to follow.

"Come, let's help Solly get through the evening. In the months ahead we will all need each other."

I walk back into the main room with her words swirling around in my head. *You deserve a good future.* The problem is,

Rivka and I have very different ideas about my good future. And really, why does that even matter? It's not like there's some nice boy out there waiting for me. The best I've been able to do is to print out a picture of Fredy Hirsch with his shirt off and fantasize about us meeting in some alternative universe.

Back at the refreshment table, I stuff two of the rugelach into my mouth and look up at the whiteboard tally. With only three precincts left to report, it's clear that Solly is out of the running.

A very dejected-looking Hannah walks over and stands next to me. I pick up the plate of rugelach and offer it to her.

"Here, drown your sorrow in chocolate. It never fails to work for me."

The room goes quiet, and when I turn my attention back to the whiteboard, I see that there is only one precinct left to report in. Solly is standing on a chair so that he can be seen by everyone in the room. Dressed in a button-down white shirt and navy pants, his *tzitzi* hanging over his side pockets, he always makes me think of the strongman Sampson without the need for the long hair. His sleeves are rolled up to his elbows and the strength in his forearms and hands is clearly visible.

Before he can speak, the room bursts into spontaneous applause and a chant of "Soll-y, Soll-y!" rings out. Hannah has her hands cupped around her mouth like a megaphone. I am clapping wildly and stamping my feet.

He is smiling at us and lowers his hands in front of him asking us to be quiet. Then he points up to the whiteboard. "I have just telephoned Barak Rausch to congratulate him on his victory."

There's a groan of "Nooooo" followed by boos, mine one of the loudest.

"Now, now," he continues, nodding, "we must respect the democratic process while we still have it."

He looks down and pauses, possibly to let that last thought sink in. Then his smile returns, and he continues. "There are so many people I have to thank for all the hard work you have done these few past months. I want all of you to know that the end of this campaign is not the end of the struggle. It is instead the beginning."

There's a smattering of applause.

"The challenges ahead are many, and each of us will be called upon to meet them in our own ways. Sometimes, like tonight, we will experience setbacks. But I know as sure as I'm standing here talking to you that Hashem will always come to the aid of those who believe in real freedom and in justice, and in the teachings of our Torah. We must stay strong and remain together as *b'nei yisrael,* the children of Israel."

And then he launches into a string of Hebrew and ends with a simple, "Thank you all."

Hannah's voice is in my ear. "I didn't catch all of the Hebrew. I think it was a psalm, right?"

Given how inattentive I am in school and synagogue, I sometimes surprise myself when I realize how much has seeped into my brain when I was preoccupied with staring at Isaac or thinking about how I might program a hologram.

As I respond to Hannah, I look around the room at the familiar faces of Binyamin Fine, Rivka Blau, Meyer Lipsky, and my father, who has taken it upon himself to fix a folding table whose legs had become bent and loose. These are the people that Solly Herschel prayed for. This is the crew, along with Judith and Isaac, who will be our best hope.

I keep looking at them as I answer Hannah's question.

"It was the end of Psalm Five. 'And let all who take refuge in You rejoice; may they ever shout for joy, and You shall shelter them, and let all who love Your name exult in You. For You, O Lord, shall bless the righteous; You shall encompass him with will like a shield.'"

CHAPTER TWENTY-SEVEN

Judith

I'm up early these days so I can use the iBrain when it goes on at six a.m. I set my alarm for five fifteen, making sure the volume is low so I don't wake up anyone else. Luckily, with Shuli married, I now have the bedroom to myself, at least until my mother decides it's time to rearrange the house and move my little sister in with me.

I've hidden the iBrain in the basement among my papercutting supplies in the back of the wooden table I use to make my art. It's in a light blue cloth sack; the exact same type that holds my X-Acto knives.

The first time I used the iBrain I felt like I was going crazy when I suddenly heard a voice in my head that wasn't mine. Jeffrey warned me this would happen, but nothing could have prepared me for what felt like an intruder inside me. That first morning, the voice was deep and sonorous, way too much like my father's. But to my great relief it disappeared after I gave the iBrain a name, as it had instructed me to do.

She is Giza, named for Giza Frankel who revived the art of Jewish papercutting in the last century. She has a sweet and pleasant voice. Jeffrey, of course, calls his Fredy. Hannah's is Esther for the Jewish Queen who saved our people from the dreaded Haman. And Isaac chose Akiba, the great rabbi who became a martyr at the hands of the Romans and died with the words of the Sh'ma on his lips. *Adonai eloheinu, Adonai echad.* Hear O Israel, the Lord is our God, the Lord is One.

I tiptoe down to the basement hoping anyone who sees me will just figure I'm up early to work on my art. Seated at my table, I fit the iBrain to the side of my head above my ear and speak quietly. "Giza, good morning." I can't help greeting her before giving her orders. She's become like a person to me.

"Good morning Judith." There she is, sweet and perky. It means nothing to her to start the day at six a.m.

"Please open my group."

The next thing I hear are voices, almost like I am on a conference call. It's Solly, speaking in a strict tone to Hannah.

"You shouldn't go down there, Hannah, it's not safe. I'm only going to make sure no one finds the iBrain if it survived."

"I'm going," she says in what I recognize as her most resolute voice. "I can help you look." Something must have happened.

"Hello? It's Judith. Survived what? And what isn't safe?"

"A bomb went off in the Federation office last night," Hannah says. Then she whispers, her voice breaking. "Rivka Blau was killed."

The words fail to penetrate for a few seconds. And then they do. "Oh my God, oh my God."

"Judith." This is Solly now. "Please try to convince Hannah not to go down to the area. We don't know what else might happen."

My elbows are on the table and I have my head in my hands. A bomb. Rivka Blau dead. Hannah's words just keep repeating and repeating, blocking out the other voices. I sit like that for a long moment until I make the connection that inevitably comes to me. Binyamin, Dani's brother.

"Professor Fine. Is he all right?"

"SJ?" It's Jeffrey. Hearing his voice has the effect of calming me. I can already feel my heart rate slowing. "My parents and I are going to the Fines' this morning. They'll need people around them to get through the next week. Can you go over there?"

"Yes," I tell him knowing that after the funeral Miriam will have to sit shiva for her sister. People will bring them food, but they'll need help with the children and keeping house. And then there are also Rivka's children; the older ones will observe the mourning period, but the younger ones will need attention.

I have no idea, once they hear about the bombing, if my parents will even let me out of the house. But I have to go. Yet I have this nagging feeling, this urge that I first have to go somewhere else. But where?

"Judith?" says Hannah. "It wasn't only the bomb, though that was the worst of it. The cemetery was vandalized, rocks were thrown through the windows of your father's office. I want you to be prepared for when he tells your family."

"Is he…?"

"The office was empty," says Jeffrey talking over me.

"*Baruch Hashem*," I whisper, and a sob escapes me, tears sting my cheeks. My father is all right, but Rivka, Rivka is dead.

"We have to stick together just like Solly said after the election," says Jeffrey.

"Isaac contacted me earlier," says Hannah. "His father went to check on the synagogue. It wasn't harmed."

"Yet," says Jeffrey. "We can't take anything for granted."

"You're right," Solly responds, his voice clear and strong. "I'm signing off. I expect I'll see you all at the funeral and at the shiva."

"I'm also going now," says Hannah, just as clear and strong as Solly.

I know that Hannah doesn't just mean she's leaving the conversation. She's going to the Federation and nothing anyone can say to Queen Esther is going to change that.

"SJ, you okay? Will I see you at the Fines'?"

It suddenly occurs to me what it is that I have to do before that.

"Yes, but I need to speak to Dvorah first."

* * *

I think about taking the iBrain with me since there's about fifteen minutes left when I can use it, but with everything going on there's a greater risk that it will be discovered. One iBrain in the wrong hands and all of us will be in great jeopardy. I carefully place it back in its little cloth sack and quietly leave the house through the basement bulkhead door. I'll have to call my mother soon so she won't worry, especially after she hears what happened last night.

I remember what Jeffrey said when he told me that he'd brought Dvorah an iBrain a week ago, and she had refused to take it, telling him she didn't feel she needed it.

"Maybe she is her own iBrain," he'd speculated. I wonder that too since Dvorah does have the power of seeing what is to come.

I don't want to wake her by coming there so early, but I can't stop myself from walking toward that simple, tidy house where so much has already been revealed. In some ways, Dvorah has become a second mother to me, providing comfort and wisdom in ways my own mother just cannot. I feel a bit guilty about that. I know my mother loves me and wants me to have a good life. It's just that I'm realizing more and more every day that her vision of the life she wants for me and the life I want for myself are moving farther and farther apart.

I knock and the door opens almost immediately. She is already dressed for the day in one of her long black skirts and a light gray long-sleeved blouse.

She nods when she sees me, almost as if I am expected. In the foyer at the bottom of the stairs, she pulls me into a hug.

"Come," she says as she lets go of me. "We'll talk over some breakfast."

When we are seated with tea and toasted bagels in front of us, Dvorah sits back in her chair and folds her arms across her chest. She is looking up at the ceiling, or possibly way beyond.

"Rivka Blau," she says at last in her faraway voice, "may her memory be for a blessing."

"*Zikhronah livrakha*," I repeat in Hebrew. "I'm going over to help out at Binyamin and Miriam's this morning."

She nods. "They will need you."

There's more silence while we both chew on bagels and sip tea. I've become used to waiting for Dvorah to speak. She's often deep in silent meditation, possibly being visited with visions of the future. I'm never sure. Maybe now all she's doing is eating. But after she drains her mug of tea, she breaks her silence.

"It pains me greatly to have to tell you, Judith, that Rivka is just the first of the deaths we will experience in days to come. I don't know who or how many, but there will be more. We must continue to honor each with our ancient mourning rituals. And also we must, in the words of a great old woman who worked for justice, 'Fight like hell for the living.'

There is a small smile on her face that acknowledges the rough language, and I smile in return.

"Will we eventually win this fight? Will the Jewish people survive?"

Dvorah covers my hand with hers and sighs. "Judith, you already know the answer to that question. The Jewish people always survive."

* * *

It is the last day of the shiva and I'm home from school to change clothes and then head over to Miriam and Binyamin's. I've been there every day, playing with the children, putting them to bed, straightening up the house. Jeffrey is there as well, joining the evening *minyan* and helping the boys with their homework.

Bernard and his children are sitting with the Fines. Binyamin explained that it was too painful for Bernard and the children to sit shiva at their house, the home that was Rivka's domain.

When I arrive, I see Binyamin sitting on one of the dining room chairs they've set up in the living room to accommodate all the people coming by. His hair is standing up and he's bent over with his face in his hands.

Solly sits next to him, a hand on his shoulder.

Binyamin turns to him, his face full of anguish. "First my job and now this? Am I on some kind of list?"

Jeffrey walks in from the hallway leading to the bedrooms and motions for me to come over.

"Do you know what's going on?" I ask him quietly as he leads me toward the children's rooms.

We stop in the hallway and Jeffrey shakes his head, closing his eyes for a second. "His latest visa application to visit his family in the UPR was declined. They told him not to bother applying again."

This is devastating news, coming so soon after the bombing. It's so unbelievable I can hardly string words together.

"But…but…why?"

Jeffrey extends his arms, palms turned up. He is still shaking his head. He flings out one arm and then the other. "Why any of this, Judith? Why are we at a shiva this week?"

"But his sister-in-law was just killed. Shouldn't they let him go see his family?"

Jeffrey sighs. "As Lipsky said to me today at school, each day, it's getting easier and easier to connect the dots. And the picture they're revealing is not a good one."

* * *

Try as we might, there is just no joy in the Sabbath this week and in the week that follows. Everywhere I go it feels like people are looking over their shoulders, waiting for the next horrible tragedy, the next act of violence. We have bombing and active shooter drills in school. My father has hired a guard to search everyone entering the newspaper's office. People are organizing into smaller *minyans* instead of taking a chance on going to the synagogue.

This past Saturday, my mother stayed home and I went to one of the small gatherings at Binyamin's. We were all there except Isaac, who felt like he had to support his father and went to the synagogue.

It is the Monday afterward and I am home helping my mother prepare our dinner. I hear the key in the door and wonder who that could be since we don't expect my father for another half hour.

"Ruchel! Ruchel! Come, we have to watch this."

My mother runs into the living room at the sound of my father's voice, the ties of her apron flaring out behind her. I follow her, worried there's been another bombing. I try to think about where Jeffrey, Hannah, and Isaac might be.

"What is all the yelling?" my mother says, also yelling.

My father has the screen remote in his hand and is rotating through the broadcast channels until he comes to one of the local news programs.

"I have a reporter at the police station. There's a press conference starting in a few minutes about the recent disruptions."

It's not the first time I've heard him use that word, disruption. It's his way of minimizing what has become a wave of antisemitic violence against us, something he refuses to acknowledge even though there's now a guard posted at the entrance to his office.

My brother and sister are in the room with us, likely wondering what my father was so upset about. He stops their questions with a "Sha, sha, just sit down and we'll all watch this together."

My mother stands and gets a look of reproach from my father. "I'm just going to turn off the burners before there's a *disruption* in this house." She says his favorite word in a bit a mocking tone. I suppress a smile.

The screen shows us a group of men, some in police uniforms, seated at a long metal table, microphones lined up in front of them. I look closely and my stomach turns at the sight of Barak Rausch seated with them. And when I scan the group a second time, I can hardly believe that Bernard Blau is sitting at the end of the table. After everything that's been happening, how can he possibly be allied with them?

My mother returns to her place on the couch just as the first speaker begins. It's our mayor, reelected the same night that

Solly lost. Even seated, he's tall and thin, his hair is mostly gray with flecks of the dark color of his youth. He begins by reviewing the events of two weeks ago—the bombing, the cemetery stones overturned and desecrated and the broken windows at the Jewish Community News. He reassures the Jewish community that the city is committed to doing everything in its power to protect us and he hopes we will give the government our cooperation in this effort.

Our cooperation? What could that even mean? Does he want *us* to find the perpetrators? Isn't that their job?

The next to speak is a uniformed man, broad-shouldered like a football player but with red ruddy cheeks that seem to sag a bit. He introduces himself as the police chief and begins by repeating the same kind of reassurances that the mayor gave us. They will do everything they can to keep us safe.

He goes on to talk about the bombing and all the other recent events, explaining that whoever did this knew how to evade the many video cameras set up in the city by wearing black ski masks, baggy black clothing and gloves. The police have so far been unable to find any evidence that would lead them to the criminals.

Then he goes on to say:

"We are, therefore, taking the following steps to keep the Jewish community of our city safe. First, we have issued an Order of Protection that asks our Jewish citizens to remain within a two-mile radius of their home neighborhood. Second, we have created a special tactical police force assigned to the Jewish neighborhood. All of the force's Jewish police have been assigned to this unit, including your new city councilor's son."

With these words, he looks over at Barak Rausch and nods at him. Barak smiles and nods back. Then the police chief turns to the camera and continues.

"The new unit will enforce the Order of Protection and issue fines to anyone who goes beyond the two-mile radius. We are doing this to ensure your protection with our limited police resources. We ask you to cooperate. Those needing to travel outside the protected area must apply for a permit and show that permit to the police in order to travel. There will be no exceptions. I now turn the mic over to your new city councilor."

Once again, Barak Rausch gives the police chief a nod and a smile and begins by thanking him and the mayor. "I want to speak directly to my Jewish community. The order of protection has been issued to ensure you are safe. We cannot go through another night like the one that killed our dear Rivka Blau of blessed memory."

He points to the end of the table. "Bernard Blau, Rivka's widower, is here with us today to assure you that he fully supports these actions by the city. There is nothing better we can do to honor Rivka's memory than to join with Bernard and myself to keep our community safe.

"I want to conclude by asking you not to listen to the troublemakers and naysayers among us who will criticize what we have done. This is not a ghetto, and there is no wall—physical or electronic—like the one at the borders with Mexico and with the UPR. Deliveries of food, medical supplies and other necessities will continue as always. We are taking these measures in the name of safety and security. I pray we will never see a night like the one a few weeks ago again."

The men rise to signal that the press conference has ended, and the voice of the news announcer comes on summarizing what we just heard. My father clicks off the screen and turns to my mother.

"All right Ruchel, now that that's over, how long till dinner?"

I stand as well, my body shaking. "Wait Papa," I plead. "Aren't we going to talk about this?"

My father, headed toward the kitchen, stops and turns to me. "What's there to talk about? Desperate times call for desperate measures. That's how I plan to frame this in the paper."

He's already written tomorrow's editorial in his head. Be good Jewish citizens and listen to the mayor. Obey the police. Don't make trouble and trouble won't find you. Desperate times.

I open my mouth to respond, but can't find any words that wouldn't violate the commandment to honor my father.

My little brother Morty, who plays the cello beautifully and hopes to one day join the Cincinnati Symphony Orchestra, looks as if he's about to burst into tears. "Judith, does this mean no more concerts?" He knows the Music Hall is more than two miles away from our neighborhood.

I draw him into a hug and kiss the top of his head. "No," I tell him. "Papa will get a permit."

A permit from the government so a Jewish child can listen to a classical music concert while a Christian child is free to go without anyone's permission but his parents'. And my father thinks this is acceptable?

I skip dinner and to my great relief my mother doesn't argue. I'm counting the hours until I can use the iBrain. It's a rare occasion where I don't even want to go down to the basement and work on a papercut. I get a little homework done and pick up a book, but end up reading and rereading the same page without taking in the meaning of the words. There's just no diversion that can transport me from this frightening reality.

I get ready for bed and lie under my quilt wondering how each of my friends has reacted to this news. Hannah I'm sure is furious and like me is counting not the hours but the minutes, knowing her, until she can use the iBrain. Isaac is nervous and is worried about Hannah and his own father. Jeffrey may be wondering why he didn't escape with Dani when he had the chance. Likely he's rethinking his decision to emulate Fredy Hirsch.

And what about me? I also had the chance to escape with Dani. Do I regret not going with her? My mind is filled with a complicated jumble of emotions made even more confusing by today's developments. Is there any way to live a Jewish life in the UPR in the way I know is right for me? Would they understand my art? What would it mean to be there with Dani? Would we, could we be more than friends? Is that what I want after the experience of kissing her?

Dvorah says Dani is my *bashert*, and since I have no reason to question anything Dvorah tells me, I'm still not sure what that would mean for us. Could we have a home together? A family?

It's all so outside the realm of what I know to be possible, but then so is my reality here. I toss around in bed, lying on one side and then the other, counting down from one hundred to zero, creating a papercut in my head, returning to thoughts of Dani and the feel of her hands on me.

Finally, I sleep for the few hours until my five fifteen alarm wakes me, and I rush down to the basement.

When I attach the iBrain and greet Giza she responds that the Owl has added two new features to the device.

"Do you want me to tell you about them?"

I respond that I do and am filled with relief at the thought that Dani's friend Julia is still working to help us. The first feature is welcome news. A second hour of what she calls "connectivity" has been added—eight to nine p.m.—which means we won't have to wait until the morning to review the day's events with one another.

The second new feature will allow us to upload, encrypt, and read files, including photographs. I'm not yet sure how this will be useful but I'm certain that Jeffrey and Meyer will figure it out.

I ask to be connected to my group and join an ongoing conversation. There's a voice I don't recognize—a woman speaking in an accent similar to people from southern GFS states. Maybe she's one of the Federation leaders that Rivka trusted.

"Yes, they've done that to us too. No one comes off our islands without a permit."

I interrupt to let them know I'm there. Binyamin greets me.

"Judith, we're speaking with Queen Olivia of the Gullah-Geechee Nation. Her people are one of the communities still in the GFS who are descendants of African slaves."

I hadn't realized there were any Black people still left here. We were taught in school that they had all left for the UPR after The Split.

"I-I don't understand. You're not in the UPR?"

"No," she responds. "My people could never leave our lands. They are what define our culture and our livelihood."

They are another community, like ours, that holds dear to its culture. I want to know more about them and why their land is so important, but Binyamin starts talking.

"Judith, Queen Olivia received an iBrain from the Federation representative in South Carolina. Her community lives on an island off the coast. They've done an incredible job of keeping the rising ocean from flooding their lands out of existence. My mother studied their methods many years ago and she'd be so glad to hear they're still thriving."

"Yes, we are," she replies, "and under more and more trying circumstances. We're so grateful to have this new technology from you and to be part of this network."

"We're also grateful to have you here. You have much to teach us," says Binyamin.

"Ah, and you us as well. We look forward to many productive conversations. I'm going to close the device now."

I wasn't sure if anyone else had been listening until I hear Solly's voice. "So we will meet at Dvorah's at seven thirty tonight?"

"Can you do that, Judith?" asks Binyamin.

"I think so. Is this to discuss what was announced yesterday?"

"Among other things," says Solly.

"See you then, SJ." This is the first I've heard from Jeffrey. I had no idea he was even there.

* * *

I'm one of the first to arrive. Dvorah opens the door and I see Binyamin and Miriam are already there with one of the Blau children, the eldest girl.

"Judith, I believe you've met my niece Naomi?" he says.

Miriam's arm is around Naomi's shoulders and the same sparkle of a good soul I saw at the shiva presents itself to me again. She's tall and thin with short, wavy honey-colored hair, a striking resemblance to her mother. I wonder how many times she's had to hear that, and how painful it must have been these last few weeks.

We have little chance to speak because Binyamin takes me aside. "Judith, I'd like to talk to you privately before the others arrive."

Dvorah nods at him and gestures toward the kitchen as if she knows exactly what he's going to tell me. It's possible that she just might know without Binyamin having to utter a single word.

The smell of brewed coffee greets us and I notice a few platters of pastries assembled for the guests. I smile to myself. Jeffrey will be happy.

Binyamin leads me to the back of the kitchen and leans an arm against the counter. "I want you to know that I'm in contact with my family. The government hasn't shut off my email so I can still contact an academic colleague in North Ohio who passes my messages along to my mother's university account. I'm using the code you and Hannah developed and they're able to send me those pixie holograms that you and Jeffrey get."

I smile and nod. "This is wonderful news. I was so upset when I heard you won't be able to travel there anymore."

"Yes, that was devastating, which is why I'm taking this chance to stay in touch, and I have you to thank for that."

I tilt my head in confusion. "Me?"

"Your code."

I think he's letting that compliment sink in because he's quiet. But his expression of pride and gratitude comes through, so I do let it sink in.

"The other thing I wanted you to know, Judith, is that Dani told me what occurred between you two when you met."

My hand flies to my mouth in surprise. What must he think of me? What must he think of Dani? Had he known about her before?

My anxiety fades when he smiles.

"You have nothing to worry about. I have known for a while that Dani is gay and I don't believe it's wrong. Things are very different in the UPR when it comes to that. Better."

"Yes. I know." It's all I'm capable of saying because I'm still very unsure what that could mean for me.

"She cares about you and is worried about your safety. But also, Judith, she believes in you and in Jeffrey. She called you both warriors." He chuckles at that and I let out a little giggle.

A warrior is the last thing I am. "She can be a bit dramatic," he says.

He reaches toward me and then retracts his hand. I imagine he's had to change quite a bit since he was raised in the more permissive environment of the UPR.

"But I agree with my sister, Judith, because I believe in you as well. You and your friends are definitely up for what lies ahead of us, whatever that is."

He motions toward the living room and we walk back to join the others. I can hear a number of voices in conversation. Dvorah passes us, heading toward the kitchen. Her smile is an acknowledgment that she's happy about our conversation. I guess I'm happy as well, maybe more like relieved. Everyone has now arrived, and I have no time to really think about any of it.

Jeffrey is sitting next to me on one of the blue couches, chewing too loudly. I poke him. "Shhh, chew quieter." He gulps down whatever is in his mouth and shrugs. "Sorrr-ry," he tells me in a way that conveys that he's not at all sorry.

Naomi is sitting with us and Hannah and Isaac are on the other couch with Solly. Meyer is in his wheelchair next to them and Dvorah and Miriam are in the two matching armchairs. Binyamin stands against the mantel over the fireplace.

"I believe we all know one another, except I should say a few words about Naomi."

Instead Naomi stands and speaks before he has a chance to continue. "Uncle Binyamin, I'd like to be the one to do that, if it's all right with you?"

He nods and his small smile is what I now recognize as an expression of pride.

Her voice starts out a little wobbly but then very quickly she finds her confidence. "I-I know some of you are surprised to see me here and maybe a little concerned after seeing my father on that broadcast last night." She pauses and looks from person to person seated around her. Her resemblance to Rivka is not just confined to her looks. She has inherited her mother's bearing, her confidence, and poise.

"I love my father, but I don't agree with how he sees things. Before she was…murdered, my mother confided in me about what was really happening."

She wipes at an eye which had been tearing up and then takes a big breath and lets it out. "I know I'm only twelve, but I'm being forced to grow up very fast. And I want to be part of what you're doing. I remember every word my mother said about this. Your cause was her cause and now it is mine. I honor her memory by joining you."

She sits down. There is silence in her wake and then a rush toward her by Miriam and Dvorah, pulling her up and hugging her. "She'd be so proud," Miriam tells her, her voice cracking. Hannah looks at me and we both rise to welcome Naomi, to what I am uncertain, but I'm grateful that Rivka's spirit is present in her daughter.

Solly stands next to Binyamin and speaks next. "In our view, the so-called Order of Protection is the first step toward getting Jews out of the GFS. None of us knows whether they mean to ultimately deport us, or worse. The acts of violence, which may have started out as random attacks by individual antisemites, are now orchestrated and targeted. We know that because no perpetrators have ever been apprehended."

He turns toward Isaac, who nods. I see Hannah lean a bit more in his direction while maintaining a small amount of space between them.

"There's no legal recourse we have against the Order of Protection," says Binyamin. "Unlike the former USA, our country does not have a strong federal constitution or a Bill of Rights. The GFS is a states' rights nation and that means that we are bound by the laws of South Ohio, which will always affirm the state's interest in maintaining security."

To my surprise, Dvorah stands and joins Solly and Binyamin. I realize in that moment that she has been planning this meeting with them.

"Up until now," she begins, "I have tried to be supportive without taking any public stands. I even refused the offer of an iBrain, although Jeffrey was quite persuasive."

Jeffrey slides down in his seat and provides the moment of comic relief that we all needed.

"But in light of these horrifying, new developments, I have reconsidered. I will take that iBrain, Mr. Schwartz."

She beams at him and he salutes in response. She looks down for a few seconds, and then, with the utmost seriousness, continues. "My father, Rabbi Josef Kuriel, may his memory be for a blessing, encouraged religious Jews to settle in this country. He believed we would be free to worship and build community in the ways of our people. I believe that in the long run what he saw of the future was not our destruction but our strength and resilience, because it is what I also see."

She looks over at Binyamin standing next to her, indicating that he should speak.

He says, "Before we begin to plan our response, I would like us to join together as a *minyan*."

Everyone looks around the room in confusion. There are only five men among us instead of the ten required for prayer.

Isaac is on his feet. "Everyone, listen," he says in a loud voice that reminds me of his father. "Binyamin has called us to pray. I know you're wondering, how can we when there are only five of us. But look around the room and you'll see that we are ten, five men and five women. We are a *minyan* and can pray together."

Hannah is smiling as she stands next to him. "A *minyan* of resistance," she announces.

"Wow," says Jeffrey. "I'm almost excited to pray."

"And we can all sit together?" asks Naomi.

"Yes," says her aunt. "It is a new day for us, for all of us."

"Isaac, will you do us the honor of leading this *minyan* of resistance in prayer?" asks Binyamin.

I remember Jeffrey saying he didn't understand why Isaac did not want to study to become a rabbi. I muse on that as Isaac leafs through his copy of the prayer book that Dvorah has distributed to each of us, instructing us to face east and then begins with the singing of *Hinei Ma Tov*—how good it is for brothers and sisters to sit together in unity—before taking us through a sequence of prayers, ending with the Kaddish so that Miriam, Binyamin, and

Naomi can stand for the traditional prayer during what is still their thirty-day period of mourning.

When he says, "And now we turn to the Kaddish," Jeffrey does the sweetest thing I have ever seen him do. He stands up and motions for Miriam to switch seats with him so that she can stand as mourner with her niece. Dvorah catches my eye and I know she is as filled with love for him as I am.

After, there is the prayer over the wine, and coffee and cake, just like after a service in synagogue. Dvorah is deep in conversation with Binyamin and Solly for a while until she asks us all to assemble again.

"This must be when we figure out just what it is this *minyan* of resistance is going to do," Jeffrey whispers to me, a bit of his usual cynical tone creeping through. He has managed to regain his original seat next to me.

"During the shiva at my home," begins Binyamin, "some members of the board of the Federation approached me and asked if I would take over Rivka's role on the staff. I was honored and a bit intimidated at the prospect of leading such an important agency. But I agreed to do so. This morning when I met the board at the Federation's temporary office, Barak Rausch was there. He informed me that the city had placed the Federation under his jurisdiction as district councilor and the offer to me was being rescinded."

Everyone begins talking at once. Hannah is so angry she is virtually jumping out of her skin. "He's an ogre!" she exclaims.

"No, ogres are nicer," Jeffrey responds, again earning smiles and nods from a few of us, including me.

When we are quiet again, Binyamin continues. "So, given these actions, the ten of us must form the core of our own federation. We will join with those around the country who are part of Rivka's Independent Jewish Network as well as with the Gullah-Geechee people of the southeast coast and all others who are sincere about wanting to be part of this struggle."

"Who are these Gullah…uh, what was it?" asks Meyer.

"Gullah-Geechee nation," Binyamin responds. "They are people of African descent who live in the GFS. I can explain more about them later. Their representative was provided an iBrain and we are in contact. They will be valuable allies to us."

Meyer looks a bit doubtful but he lets Binyamin continue.

"If you all agree, Dvorah, Solly and I would like to become members of a four-person governing council. The rest of you will be part of what we will call The First Minyan of Resistance, in hopes that there will be others. It will be easier for just four of us to consult, strategize and plan instead of all ten."

"Uncle Binyamin, who is the fourth member of the, what did you call it?"

"The governing council, Naomi. We were thinking it would be Isaac."

Isaac sits with one hand shielding his eyes as if he is once again praying. Then he shakes his head. "While I appreciate the invitation, I'm not the right person. I want instead to lead the *minyan* when we pray, just like I did a little while ago. The person you need up there with you is Hannah."

She looks at him, her mouth open in surprise.

"There is no one I know who is braver, smarter, and has more integrity. She is your fourth leader."

He looks at her and gives her a nod of encouragement, and to my complete and utter amazement, she reaches over and hugs him, breaking with tradition. It is likely the first time they have touched.

Isaac's eyes are open in astonishment, but then he places his arms on her shoulders and hugs her back.

Jeffrey leans over and whispers to me, "Well SJ, now they're just like you and me."

I rear back and shake my head.

"I don't mean like that," he says. "I mean, you know, they broke the touching barrier."

"The touching barrier?"

"Oh, you can be so difficult sometimes, SJ."

That comment earns a smile from me and a shake of my head.

Hannah has joined the others standing in front of the fireplace, and I can see as they face us that she was indeed the right choice. Dvorah squeezes her shoulder and keeps her hand there. They will undoubtedly grow closer.

I sit back on the couch wondering what all of this means for me. Will the special relationship I have with Dvorah now fade in favor of Hannah? What can I possibly contribute here to this resistance? I stay seated when Jeffrey walks across the room to talk to Meyer and Isaac, and Naomi is over with her aunt.

Who is Judith Braverman in all of this? When I ask myself that question, nothing at all comes to mind. I squeeze the bridge of my nose with two fingers to stop the tears from coming.

When I look up, Dvorah is standing over me.

"Judith, please help me clean up."

Miriam has begun stacking cups and plates, but Dvorah stops her. "Let me do this with Judith," she says.

When we're both loaded down with the remains of the coffee and pastries, we move to the kitchen.

I place everything on the counter and Dvorah takes my hand and leads me to the kitchen table.

"Tell me why you are sad," she says. She has placed both of her hands over mine.

I look at the checkerboard pattern of the yellow and white kitchen curtains that frame the window over the sink, and this time I am unable to stop the tears. "There's nothing I can do to help. I'm not brave like Hannah, or good with the device like Jeffrey and Meyer. Maybe there's someone else who should be…" And I'm unable to keep talking because I am sobbing.

Dvorah's hands are now resting on my shoulders. "Judith, look at me."

I've been avoiding doing just that, but I force myself to look into her earnest, soft green eyes.

"Your gifts are so critical to this struggle."

"Because I can see the *neshamah*?" I ask through my sniffles.

"Yes, but not just that." She hands me a few white napkins sitting in a holder on the table. "Put yourself together and then come back in with me. I want to show you something. Give me just a minute or two."

She leaves me sitting in the kitchen. I'm hoping she's not telling the others that I've been crying. I especially don't want Binyamin and Solly to see me this way, weak and emotional.

I blow my nose, wipe my tears, and decide I should wash my face to help fade the red blotches on my cheeks, I hope.

I slowly walk into the living room and Dvorah has turned on the screen that sits on the little table where she first introduced us to Fredy Hirsch and the other Jewish men who were gay. Everyone has left except Binyamin, Solly, and Hannah. They stand with Dvorah looking at the screen.

When I walk over, I see words in white against a black background. *Silence=Death*. Below is a small triangle in pink.

"In the last century, there was a plague called AIDS that killed hundreds of thousands of gay men, among others," she explains. "In the early years, the government took little notice of the epidemic because it was affecting a population that it didn't value. So a movement arose, and this poster with this slogan was carried in demonstrations and glued onto building walls. It became a battle cry that helped more and more people realize that things had to change."

She touches the screen and a second image appears. "This is a quilt that was part of the protest in Washington, DC against the government's inaction on AIDS. But it was also a memorial. Each square was made by friends and family of those who had died." In the picture, the quilt laid out on the grounds of a large park with a tall, thin white monument in the background.

She pauses so we can all look at the very moving image of the quilt.

"There's a lot more I can say about this, but I'd like to show you one more thing."

Again, she's touching the screen. We're now looking at a drawing. An artist is sitting at his table, pen in hand. On the paper in front of him is what looks like a three-dimensional Adolf Hitler, come to life from the artist's hand, though his feet are still not yet off the page. Hitler is on his back, trying not to fall off the end of the table. Another Nazi stands atop a second piece of paper to the right of the artist. He is also perilously close to the edge of the table. There are Nazis in uniform strewn all over the floor, as if they had been discarded by the artist. It is funny and also quite disturbing to see all that evil in one picture.

"This was drawn by the Jewish artist Arthur Szyk, originally from Poland." Dvorah turns away from the screen and looks right at me. "He called himself 'a Jew praying in art.' Here's another of his."

This is a drawing in pencil or black ink. Three Jewish children are huddled together, armbands with the Star of David attached to their sleeves. Barbed wire wound around wooden fencing surrounds them. There is so much emotion in their expressions, you want to just reach out and hug them.

Dvorah touches the screen and it turns off. "You see, Judith, artists have always been important members of resistance movements especially when lives were at stake. Your talent will be just as valuable to this struggle as Meyer Lipsky's ability to reverse engineer an iBrain."

As she speaks images begin to come to me of a map measuring a two-mile radius and a permit with a giant black Aleph over it, looking almost like an X.

"Art will inspire and sustain us, and provide comfort when times are hardest," says Binyamin.

"So start drawing! The governing council needs its own Arthur Szyk," Hannah tells me and bumps my shoulder with hers. We face each other and grin.

"Okay," I say to all of them.

But before I walk out the door, I take in the four of them, huddled together again in conversation. Together they make the perfect leaders for our *Minyan of Resistance*, the core of the new Independent Jewish Network.

Solly is the strength.

Dvorah is the spirit.

Hannah is the courage.

And Binyamin. My *bashert's* brother. He is the heart.

Other Books by Cindy Rizzo

Novels
Getting Back
Love Is Enough
Exception to the Rule

Short-Fiction & Essays
Language of Love
Conference Call
Our Happy Hours: LGBT Voices from the Gay Bars
Love Times Two
Unwrap These Presents
All the Ways Home

About the Author

Cindy Rizzo is the award-winning author of three novels and a number of published short stories and essays, plus one peer-reviewed paper in a professional journal. In 2014, she won the Debut Author award from the Golden Crown Literary Society. She has had a long and satisfying career in philanthropy and currently leads the LGBTQ Social Justice Program at the Arcus Foundation. In 2019, she received the Reid Erickson Trailblazing Leadership Award from Funders for LGBTQ Issues. Cindy has had the pleasure of serving on multiple community boards and is currently a member of the board of SAGE, the country's only national organization advocating for and serving LGBT seniors. She is also a member of Congregation Beit Simchat Torah in New York City. Cindy and her wife, Jennifer, have two adult sons and three granddaughters. They live in Manhattan with their three cats.

Acknowledgments

It did not begin with the election of 2016, this splitting of red and blue that's moved us farther and farther apart. It may have always been present in some form. But the advent of cable television, which created new and myriad options for letting us sort ourselves into our preferred entertainment and news channels, followed by the Internet—which encouraged us to both remain in our own echo chambers and forsake all manner of civil discourse when we ventured out of them—accelerated it.

Evidence of polarization and the distrust and hatred it spawned can be found in many places. One stark statistic I came across as I began to research this book was the growth of what are known as "landslide counties,"—counties in which one major Presidential candidate defeated the other by at least 20 percent. In 1992, 38 percent of voters lived in one of these counties. But by 2016, 60 percent did. Clearly, over the last few decades, we in the US have been engaging in what journalist Bill Bishop has dubbed The Big Sort.

It isn't therefore too much of a reach to imagine the US ultimately sorting itself into two separate countries, which is what The Split series imagines.

I have many people to thank who helped me move this book from concept to completion. Chief among them is Linda Hill, the Publisher of Bella Books. I pitched this book to Linda a few years ago and her enthusiasm and support of me and the novel was more than I could have expected or asked for. When it came time to submit the book, I knew Linda and her team would give it their loving attention, and they have. Publishing with Bella also gave me the privilege and honor of working with Katherine V. Forrest as my editor. An iconic romance, science fiction, and mystery author, and experienced editor, Katherine pointed out so many places where I could strengthen the book. She also identified key aspects of the world building that needed my attention. Any author who's worked with her knows that it's a bit daunting to open one of Katherine's "letters" detailing everything you need to work on in the next draft. I took a quick peek at mine and then was too intimidated to start my revisions until Katherine emailed me two weeks later with much needed encouragement.

My beta readers flagged so many important issues and made really helpful suggestions. Thanks to Stefani Deoul, an accomplished young adult author in her own right; my dear friend across The Pond, Clare Ashton, whose exquisite writing I can only hope one day to emulate; and my dear friend, Ann Roberts, a prolific and wonderful author and editor who not only read the first draft but listened patiently to all of my dilemmas. Her advice: "these things have a way of working themselves out" was just what I needed to hear at a critical point in time. Finally, my friend and fellow writer and queer philanthropoid, Ben Francisco Maulbeck, urged me to pay more attention to the fate of people of color in the God Fearing States and suggested I learn more about the partition of India to gain a greater understanding of what happens when a nation is pulled apart. His recommendation led me to read the novel *Partitions* by Amit Majmudar, a beautifully written and heartbreaking account of the lives of Hindu, Sikh, and Muslim characters during that tumultuous and violent time.

It's always tricky to get through that middle part of any book you are writing, and I was fortunate enough to spend a week writing at Wellspring House, a retreat in Ashfield, Massachusetts, where I spent hours each day writing and getting myself to a place where I could envision what needed to be done to get to the end.

My ability to write about Judaism and Jewish themes is a testament to my mother, Betty Goldstein Rizzo, whose memory to me will always be a blessing. She was adamant that I be raised Jewish and I am so grateful to her, as well as to both my father, Felix, for agreeing to that, and my step-sister Rosealice D'Avanzo, a devout Catholic, who has always encouraged my devotion to Judaism. While my specific path has included twists and turns and an occasional cul de sac, I am thankful that I learned to love Judaism from the Jewish lesbian community in

Boston in the 1980s; from the LGBT Jewish community, Am Tikva; from Temple Israel of Boston where I had my adult bat mitzvah; and most recently from Congregation Beit Simchat Torah in New York City with its brilliant and visionary leader Rabbi Sharon Kleinbaum.

In the end, this book could not have been written without the loving support and encouragement of my wife, Jennifer, who listened to multiple readings and always gave me her honest opinion. I'm sure if I ever run into someone like Dvorah Kuriel and tell her about my wife, she will gasp, smile and tell me that I have surely met my very own *bashert*.

Bella Books, Inc.

Women. Books. Even Better Together.

P.O. Box 10543
Tallahassee, FL 32302

Phone: 800-729-4992
www.bellabooks.com